C000174340

A *Dire Wolves* MISSION

Savage Silence

A Dire Wolves MISSION

ELLIS LEIGH

Kinship Press

Savage Silence: A Dire Wolves Mission
Copyright © 2016 by Ellis Leigh

First Edition

ISBN
978-1-944336-18-9

Kinship Press
P.O. Box 221
Prospect Heights, IL 60070

Throw away thy rod, throw away thy wrath;
O my God, take a gentle path.

— GEORGE HERBERT

One

His paws pounding against the rocky ground beneath him, Thaus raced along a jagged cliff. A cold rain misted over the forest, quieting the fauna until there was nothing but his breaths, his footfalls. Him.

Noise killed. Of that, Thaus was convinced. When constantly barraged with the cacophony of human life in a city, he could almost feel the tenacious train toward death begin to roll. The sounds would build, piling high on his psyche in a mountain of nothing but input, until his inner wolf slowly dimmed. Until the presence of the beast within quieted in a way that made his human side actually feel the slow drag toward the end. The release from the animal who'd shared his mind since birth felt as much like a death as anything else could, more even. He should know. He'd survived far longer than anyone should have and technically had been dead more times than he could remember. He'd hopped on and off that train a few times.

But one of the benefits of being a Dire Wolf shifter was

regeneration. Death could come calling day after day, but Thaus and his wolf would walk away from that edge and return to their life. There had been a time or two—or five—where they couldn't walk back. Times where the damage done had been too great, the injuries too extreme to get up and shake it off. At those times, he'd been carried by the other Dire Wolves, rescued and ferreted away someplace safe and quiet until he healed. That's what brotherhood was about—no man fought alone, and no one got left behind. That noisy train of death wasn't taking one of his six pack-mates, for they were the last of the breed, the final Dires left on earth. And they were far more stubborn than death itself.

But the noise…the cars and sirens, the constant talking and endless screeching and creaking of vehicles. It was all too much. Modern life of humans wore on the ancient shifter. When Thaus needed an escape, when the humanity of city life grew to be too much for his wolf spirit, he sought silence in the great forests of the Pacific Northwest. Where tall trees and even taller mountains ruled the scene, where most humans didn't dare to explore, and where his wolf was happiest.

Thaus ran faster, hugging the precipice, his eyes locked on a deer. His prey ran on a parallel path below him, running hell-bent toward a thicket of trees he probably thought he could get lost in, looking to escape. That wouldn't happen, though. Thaus knew this range better than anyone else. He knew every crag and valley, every path and goat trail. The Pacific Northwest was his home in many ways, and these mountains his playground. He'd beat the little deer racing toward its own death without really trying, simply because he was better prepared to take on the terrain.

As the trail dipped lower, Thaus spotted his chance. He quickened his steps, letting his wolf come fully forward, giving the animal the reins of their shared mind so he could relish the hunt. Knowing his opportunity was coming. And then his chance presented itself, just as he'd known it would. The deer slipped on the pebbly ground, stumbling twice before regaining its footing. The last mistake it ever had a chance to make. Thaus growled and leapt, back claws scattering stones as he pushed off the edge of the ridge. He landed on the back of the deer with enough force to roll the thing far off the trail, coming out on top when they finally slid to a stop. But Thaus released the gentle creature, content in a successful hunt without the kill. Besides, he liked his food a little more well-done.

Hours later, after a long run through the woods and a dip in the stream to clean his fur, Thaus padded up the steps to the little cabin tucked deep in the shadows of the tall pines. The place wasn't anything special—just some old hunting lodge he'd come upon one summer—but it was the one location he considered his den. His home. Plain old his.

Thaus had made a few changes over the years, of course, adding things like satellite dishes and electricity to run his appliances. He had no phone line. Though, with the invention of reliable cell phones, he didn't feel he needed one. Besides, this place was his escape. His safe place. He'd rather not have rings and pings disturbing his silence.

As if on cue, the cell phone on the kitchen counter rang right as he nosed his way inside. Figured. Thaus growled low in his throat, not ready to face the outside world, but knowing his packmates wouldn't bother him if they didn't need to. He wasn't exactly the pack sounding board, after all.

Thaus shifted human just before he hit the old, knotted rug he'd purchased from a native woman decades before, stumbling at the pain in his shoulder as he morphed from one form to another.

"What?" he grunted as soon as he swiped to pick up the call.

"We have a mission for you, Dire Thaus."

Dante. Of course. Mate to the political leader for North

American shifters, the man doled out missions to the Dire Wolves on a regular basis. Things his private police-type forces couldn't handle. Things no one wanted to deal with. Thaus didn't often get called directly—usually, he would be added to a mission assigned to one of his packmates. His skills and talents tended to lean toward the weaponry side of their group—stocking, building, repairing, and knowing exactly how to use everything from handguns to C-4 charges. If the brass was calling him of all the Dires, the mission would probably be one that ended in bloodshed.

"Good afternoon, Dante." Thaus rolled his shoulder to work out the ache. Fucking hell, the more time passed, the worse it got. He'd need to head back to Chicago soon, to the very building where Dante probably sat on the other end of the line, to see if the doctor could try to break it again. Perhaps realigning the bones would help with the stiffness of his shifts. "Mission instructions?"

"We're going to need you to broker a contract negotiation."

Ache forgotten, Thaus stared at the phone. Contract negotiation? That was the work of a Regional Head, some low-level political official. Not a Dire Wolf. Especially not one like Thaus.

"I'm unclear on my participation, sir."

The other man coughed a single bleat of a laugh. "I bet. I know this isn't your normal type of job, but the Glaxious pack is making a fuss, and I worry that the Alpha could cross a line. The other pack involved, the Kwauhl, have a new member. A shewolf who is now caught up in a contract for a mating claim that's over two hundred years old. The Glaxious pack refuses to release her from the contract, even though she is adamantly opposed to a forced mating."

Glaxious pack. Shit. Thaus had run into those bastards before. The pack was small if he remembered right, but the Alpha was a jackass and about as antiquated as a wolf could be. If a sought-after shewolf was involved in this dispute, Glaxious would be three times as bad as they normally were. Still...

"I'm not certain why you want me, sir."

Silence. Long and weighty, it added a tension to the conversation that Thaus could feel deep inside of him. This wasn't an ordinary case. He'd known it the second Dante had asked him to work a mission directly. Had felt it. And the drawn-out pause amplified that sense.

Dante hummed softly and took a breath that made the static on the line grow for a moment before dropping the truth. "The shewolf is an Omega."

Thaus growled deeply, unable to control the fury those words incited. Omega shewolves were the pride of any pack lucky enough to have one. Fierce, strong, and with an innate power to strengthen the ties that bound the rest of the pack members together, the women were normally honored and revered. They were also coveted, stolen, and enslaved at times. Something he'd seen with his own eyes just a handful of years before. Images he could never forget and had vowed to make sure never happened again.

That aspect made accepting the mission so much easier for the Dire. "When and where?"

"Thank you, Dire Thaus. I'll text you the coordinates. As for when, the sooner the better. The Kwauhl pack's Alpha was hesitant to call us in because of the history of this particular Omega. She needs a strong guard, to say the least."

And there it was, the reason they'd called him. He and his brothers believed all Omega females were descended from the original Dire packs, and therefore were to be treated as Dire Wolves. If this Omega needed a strong guard to settle her fears, Thaus would play that role. He'd do anything he needed to keep her safe. That was his vow—and one he took seriously.

"Understood and mission accepted. I'll leave as soon as I receive the coordinates." Without waiting for a response, Thaus hung up and stalked to the bedroom at the back of the cabin. Under the floorboards in a well-hidden cubby lay the proof of his place within the Dire pack. Pounds of explosives, guns of multiple calibers, and enough ammunition to hold off the US Army for at least a few days. As the weaponry expert of his pack, his job was to keep their safe houses armed and ready for battle. His own house was always ready, as well.

The ping of an incoming text barely registered as he counted out guns, knives, and bullets. He might hate how shifters had grown so comfortable with mechanical weapons, but he had to admit they were effective as fuck when an enemy attacked. And over the last few years, the enemies had all been heavily armed. Long gone were the days when two wolves would fight to the death with tooth and claw. It was the age of bullets and firepower, and Thaus always came prepared.

He packed everything he'd need into a specially designed backpack and headed to the kitchen to grab his phone. As expected, there was one text from Dante listing the coordinates of the pack he was to help. He stared at the screen long enough for it to go dark, trying to work out the possibilities that this was a coincidence. The pack was close. Real close. A hard half-day's run, especially with his shoulder aching, but no more than that. Out of all the places he could have been and all the packs that could have called for help, it was oddly prophetic that he was at just the right mountain for just the right pack. Not that it mattered—no one fucked with a Dire Wolf, and any Omega shewolf was a Dire, which meant the pack could have been across the country or over oceans, and Thaus would have helped. Their proximity just meant it wouldn't take as long to get started.

Once he shifted—cursing bullets and chemicals all over

again as his shoulder burned through the transition—he crawled under the strap of the backpack. The weight of his supplies was minimal, though the strap rubbed his shoulder wrong. Still, it was better than trying to travel in his human form.

He'd run onto this land with the backpack over his shoulder, and he was running back out the same way. Only for a little while, though. As soon as this contract negotiation finished, he was coming back to his mountain.

He just had to make sure the Omega was safe first.

_T_ he prick of pine needles under her paws thrilled Ariel
to no end. She'd been cooped up at work for too long,
had been spending every waking moment at the clinic orga-
nizing, seeing patients, and trying to prove her worth. Not
that she needed to—the members of her new pack had accepted her without question. Still, the drive to be useful, to
be an asset, was strong. So she'd worked tirelessly until her
Alpha had stormed into the clinic and demanded she come
for a run.

And thank the stars and the sun that he had. This was
what she needed to clear her head and allow her soul to relax.
The wind in her fur, the freedom of the woods around her,
and the presence of a pack at her side. This was as close to
feeling at home as she'd experienced in years.

Alpha Lathan raced in front of her, his head down and
tail high. He was playing a game with Ariel, letting her get
close, and then pushing himself harder to escape her teeth. It
was a game he often played with the pups in the pack to help

them train for endurance runs. Something she had told him she needed as well. Too many months being tortured had left her weak and frail in her own mind if not in her body. But no longer. She was out to heal, to forget the past and move forward, and that meant keeping up her strength. Her Alpha worked her hard, and she was grateful to him for it.

The group of wolves crested the top of a hill and came to a slow stop. A valley of trees spanned out before them, leading to the ocean miles away. Their Alpha shifted human on that hilltop, his long, black hair cascading down his muscular back. Naked and strong, the man stood staring toward the far-off horizon, looking at once powerful and so small in relation to the vastness of the forest around them. An impressive man by all rights. He'd offered himself to Ariel as a pleasure mate when she'd first arrived, but it hadn't taken long for him to realize she was far too broken for such a thing. Too broken and too afraid to be touched. So he'd taken her under his wing instead, pushed her when she needed to be pushed and supported her through her healing. She cared for him, but much in the way a child cared for a favorite teacher or coach. Nothing more. She didn't even think it was possible for her to feel *more* about a man again.

"Shift, Ariel. I want to talk to you about Glaxious," Alpha Lathan said, his calm, deep voice washing over her like a warm breeze.

The group of wolves edged away to give her room. But while the other men and women moved closer to one another, seeking out that almost constant connection they thrived off of, Ariel held back. Not separate, just…in her own space. No one pushed her, no one attempted to force their touch on her. They all knew she couldn't handle the attention. They'd all seen her fall apart at least once when someone surprised her with something as simple as a hand on her arm or a bump in the side from a fellow wolf. They knew her limits.

They'd seen the scars.

The same ones that appeared as she shifted human and took a few cautious steps toward the man waiting for her.

"The rainy season will come soon, and the mudslides will be intense," Lathan said, turning to eye his pack, giving Ariel a come-hither nod. "You ready for broken humans, Doc?"

"I'm always ready to do my job."

"We'll see." He swung his arm wide, an invitation of sorts. One she'd come to understand and know how to accept. She answered his invite by inching closer, almost close enough to feel the heat from his body. Centimeters from his touch. "Look there. See that cliff?"

Ariel did see it, and she knew something wasn't right about it even from as far away as she stood. There was a sense of unbalance to the outcropping, a darkening of the shadows that shouldn't be there. "What's wrong with it?"

"The land beneath has eroded from the forestry work. Fifty years later, and the mountainside still hasn't recovered."

The dread that knotted in her stomach took Ariel by surprise, as did the sudden knowledge of where this conversation was going. "It'll fall this season."

"Yes," her Alpha said. "And probably soon. We should make sure the campers and the humans in town all know to stay clear of the mountains to the north."

She bit her lip in an unconscious gesture, plans and strategies falling into place in her mind. "We'll need more supplies at the clinic. If humans get caught in the middle of a large-scale slide, it could be catastrophic for them. I'll need helpers as well."

"You'll have what you need."

"Thank you, Alpha." She let her mind wander, calculating worst-case scenarios and disaster preparedness models. She'd need access to the blood bank. Shifters could regenerate and take a direct infusion if need be, but humans were a different story. Without access to that bank, she might as well not open her clinic's doors. Something she refused even to think about.

She'd been a doctor for over sixty years. Having grown up in a pack with no medic had forced her hand in a way, but after six decades of caring for shifters and humans alike, she was beyond comfortable in her role. The analytic side of her job, the process of elimination and the overall organization required, was a perfect fit for her. She'd saved many lives since she'd earned her MD. Many…including her own a time or two.

"Where did you go?" Lathan asked, waving a hand in front of her face.

"Sorry. Just thinking through the plan for the clinic."

His dark eyes bored into hers, his expression one of kindness and understanding. "You want to go to the clinic for inventory, don't you?"

She tried not to let it show, but yes. Yes, she did. A run in the woods was a nice way to unwind, but the draw of plotting and planning and making sure she was prepared for the worst held far more appeal. And her Alpha knew it.

Lathan laughed, practically shooing her off the mountain. "Go, Doc. Go do what you love. The woods will be here when you're through."

"I thought you wanted to talk about the Glaxious pack."

His smile fell, his eyes going stormy. The neighboring pack had been causing trouble lately, meeting with Lathan more and more. He'd told her not to worry, but that was an impossible task. How could she not? According to her pack-mates, the Glaxious hadn't bothered with them for decades. Not until she joined.

"Another time," he said, his voice dark and rough. Measured. There was bad news coming, she could feel it. Could practically see it just like on that far-off cliff to the north. The shadows were deepening, and she'd need to be prepared for when things got dark.

"Then I guess I'll head back to the clinic to start getting the word out."

Lathan nodded, watching her with an attentiveness she could feel. If only…if only she hadn't been taken. Held hostage. Tortured. If only life could have been a little more kind.

"Be careful," he said as she turned to shift back to her wolf form. "Stay to the marked trails, and check in with Davis whenever you can."

Ariel's heart almost hurt. She was so thankful she'd run into this pack, so blessed to have found a safe place after so much fear. Lathan worked hard to accept her needs, to help her find herself, and to give her time to grow. She'd forever be grateful to him for that, but there would never be more. She would never feel his body against hers or enjoy those quiet moments between pleasure mates. And that was entirely her fault.

"Thank you," she whispered, wishing there was some way she could express how much he and his pack—their pack—meant to her. But she didn't have the words, not that Lathan seemed to need them.

"Thank you, Ariel. Now go before I change my mind and make you run back to camp the long way."

She shifted without thought, twisting into a running wolf in a single breath. She was back over the hilltop in four strides, far enough from the pack to no longer feel their presence in twenty. If she kept up that pace, she'd be at her clinic in half an hour, which suited her just fine. There was much to be done. Inventory, order supplies, contact the local blood bank—her night would be busy with tedious administrative tasks, but she liked it that way. Liked being the only doctor around for miles and miles. Liked the endless hours and the happy exhaustion that finally forced her to her bed every night. The pace kept her mind off the darker memories, kept her focused on healing instead of sinking into the quagmire of her past. Kept her wanting to move forward.

Staying busy kept her sane.

Three

The phone would be Thaus' undoing.

"So what, you're on babysitting duty for two Alphas?" Phego, his Dire brother, huffed what sounded like a sarcastic laugh.

The jackass.

"It's not babysitting." Thaus could no longer remember why he'd stopped running to place this call. He'd been so much calmer in his wolf form, without the added noise of Phego being…well, Phego.

"Sounds like babysitting to me. Is that really a Dire Wolf type of job? Bartering between two pompous asses over antiquated rules? Why didn't Dante send out the Feral Breed to handle this?"

Thaus knew exactly why. "The shewolf's an Omega."

Phego was silent for a long, tense moment before he finally breathed out a quiet, "Shit."

"Exactly," Thaus said, his voice growing louder and filling with the undertone of his growl as he continued. "Some

Alpha has it in his head that he can claim her as a mate simply because a two-hundred-year-old piece of paper says he gets to call dibs."

"Not happening." Phego's declaration was just as loud, just as rumbly. Just as strong as Thaus' had been. No one fucked with a Dire Wolf, and an Omega *was* a Dire Wolf to their team. "Dante does realize you won't really be negotiating shit, right?"

Thaus almost smiled at that. "He's not ignorant of my skills. He knew what he was getting when he chose to call me."

"Then mount up, brother. I'm heading to Los Angeles to check in on the Hollywood Feral Breed crew."

That was almost believable, but Thaus knew the man too well. "You mean, hang out on the beach."

"That, too. But seriously. I'll be close enough to help if you need me."

"Affirmative. Enjoy the sun." Thaus ended the call with a swipe and tucked the phone back into his bag. He'd run all night, racing past trees and over rock croppings most of the way. He still had a few hours to go, though he couldn't just run past this point without taking a moment to appreciate it. The view practically stole his breath—miles of trees, mountainous foothills, and way far to the north and west, the sliver of blue signifying the ocean he'd been slowly running away from. And down there, deep in the trees and even farther from that faraway ocean, sat the packlands of the Glaxious and Kwauhl. Neighbors in the forests, though how amicable, Thaus had yet to determine. But from his vantage point, everything appeared peaceful and still. He liked that. Liked the idea of being able to enjoy the silence in a group of people. So long as they left that shewolf the fuck alone.

Time to hike down there.

Donning the clothes he'd packed, he spent a few minutes getting his head ready for the ridiculousness he was sure to encounter. He would be walking onto the complaining pack's land first. He'd need to be prepared for attitude and antiquated ideals. He'd need to be prepared for anything.

What he walked into, though, was not easily prepared for.

The packlands were definitely quiet and still, though not because of any sense of peace. The pack was struggling to survive. As he walked into their camp, the lingering scents of a robust, thriving pack whispered to him. Like old pictures faded over time, the spirits and energy of members long gone left an imprint. Left the forest scarred by their presence and their loss. This had once been a strong, solid pack.

But something had changed.

Thaus could only sense eight or nine shifters on the grounds. That was too small, especially when he considered the only female scent came from a human. One with the energy imprint of someone scared and alone; someone clinging to something she thought was a life raft, but was really sinking her.

But there was more. Hidden energies and silenced voices. Somewhere close. Thaus felt surrounded, assumed he was being watched. This group was much more dangerous than a small, failing pack. This was also not a true pack; it was a band of shifters up to something very, very wrong.

"Who the fuck are you, and why are you on my land?" A man full of arrogance and anger—probably the Alpha—stalked over as Thaus walked past two hovel-like structures. Another man stepped out of the shadows of one of the dilapidated buildings, watching. Waiting to see who won the battle so he could scavenge the carcass of the fallen, no doubt. Or so he could snatch the power away from the one holding it. Thaus didn't need to know that shifter to know that look. Definitely not a pack.

Time to get to work so he could get the fuck out of

here. "I'm Cleaner Sathaus. President Blasius Zenne sent me here regarding a contract dispute."

The man watching from the sidelines barked a laugh. "He sent a Cleaner for a contract dispute? Aren't you guys supposed to be the big, bad soldiers of the NALB? You too weak to be anything more than a paper pusher, son?"

Thaus wasn't stupid enough to bite at that, though he secretly hoped he'd get the chance to show the jackass exactly how weak he wasn't. "We serve at the pleasure of our president."

The assumed Alpha sneered. "Yes, well, so long as you can read, I guess you'll do. Come on, then. I'll show you the contract."

But Thaus didn't follow orders from the likes of men like him. "And you are?"

Thaus already knew who he was, knew the guy's place in this straggly little group from the second he opened his arrogant mouth. Still, he asked for confirmation. Thaus wasn't about to give the guy the respect immediately marking him as an Alpha would impart. He'd rather piss the fucker off and keep him off-balance.

The Alpha turned slowly, his face red and his eyes angry. Score one for Team Dire.

"I am Alpha Chilton of the Glaxious Pack," the man said, obviously seething. "We have been a member of the NALB for almost three centuries and are well known throughout the leadership."

Thaus raised an eyebrow at that comment. Dire Wolves only had two levels of leadership—pack Alpha Luc and Blasius Zenne, the president they all chose to follow. And that non-pack connection with President Zenne was easy to end should the need become apparent. But this guy had no clue who or what he really was, so Thaus kept his mouth shut. Though he stared the Alpha down until the man finally broke.

Some things simply had to be done.

"Well," Chilton said, shaking off the challenge Thaus had won. "If you have no other stupid questions, we'll get this started."

Thaus followed the angry imp across the muddy ground, biting back a grin. He'd gotten under the guy's skin. Sometimes it was fun putting these so-called Alphas in their place. It'd really be fun when he told Chilton the Glaxious pack couldn't simply call claim on the Omega shewolf. If she didn't want to join the pack—and he could totally see why no woman ever would—she wasn't joining it. Period. Dante wouldn't have assigned the job to Thaus if he'd wanted some sort of compromise. No one sent a warrior to deal with paperwork unless they were ready to see the entire building where the paper was stored burned to the ground.

"Eight members, or nine?" Thaus asked, unable to figure out why he couldn't lock in on a number.

Chilton shot him a side-eye sort of look. "Eight."

"Small pack."

"My men are strong fighters. We're very blessed."

Thaus didn't see eight men living in the woods with a leader like Chilton as blessed. He also knew there were a lot more than eight shifters roaming nearby. Shifters he doubted Chilton had the power or strength to control. "And the human woman?"

"She asked to join us, so I allowed it." Chilton chuckled. "Everyone needs to burn off a little steam now and again."

Chilton's laugh, the sarcastic way he said those words, the obvious disrespect for a human life… If Thaus hadn't been on an assigned mission, he would have knocked the fucker to the ground. What a disgusting piece of shit. Thaus had no great love for the human race, but he still didn't want to see them treated as some sort of slave for the needs of multiple shifters. There was absolutely no way this guy was getting a paw on *his* Omega.

His? Thaus almost stumbled at that thought. Shit. Not *his*. The Omega wasn't his to claim. Not in any way. She was a Dire by history and blood—no more, no less.

Alpha Chilton led him into a dank, rotting wood structure at the edge of the clearing. The building—if one could call it that—reeked of mold and rot, but the other man didn't seem to notice. Thaus, on the other hand, had to fight back his inner wolf to walk even a foot inside. Something about this place unsettled the beast, not an easy thing to do.

Chilton headed straight for a large book left open on a table at the back of the room. "This is the contract, signed by the then-Alpha of the Kwauhl."

"And what happened to that Alpha?"

Chilton grinned in a way that would have sent a chill down lesser men's spines. "He met an unfortunate end during a battle for power."

Thaus doubted that, but it wasn't his place to find fault with an Alpha overturning.

"Different Alpha, different rules." Still, Thaus glanced over the document in question, eyeing the slashy signatures along the bottom.

"Same pack, same rule," Chilton replied, a slight growl to his voice. "I have a contract, and I expect it to be fulfilled."

Thaus ran a finger along the page, checking over the language and the details. Tapping on the date listed at the very top. "Why now?"

"Pardon?"

"You've had two centuries," Thaus said, backing away from a contract that probably would have passed in human courts. "Why are you attempting to enact this now?"

"They have a shewolf I want."

That wasn't the admission Thaus was looking for. "Why's that?"

"Why does any man chase a particular tail?" Chilton

said with a lazy shrug of a shoulder. "Besides, it doesn't matter. Right there in black and white it says, by giving them territory rights in the mountains, I can claim a Kwauhl shewolf for a non-fated mating. I've chosen. The shewolf is mine."

Thaus had one quick thought that the guy had yet to use the shewolf's name before the rage from Chilton's words swept over him. He wanted to punch the Alpha in the face, burn the contract, and get the fuck out of there so he could protect the shewolf. Sadly, he'd need to be a little more subtle than that. Already, he could sense the men of the pack moving closer, circling like the hungry animals he knew them to be. They were making a shifter net around the house, probably thinking they could trap him should he not do what Chilton wanted. An interesting tactic, but not one that he hadn't lived through before.

Still, he had yet to get a good read on the number of shifters not present on packlands, and fighting his way out of this shithole wasn't in Thaus' plans. Neither was doing anything that could endanger the Omega more. He needed to focus on business.

"I need to discuss this with the other Alpha."

Chilton stared, as if he'd expected more of a statement. Or simply expected Thaus to give in and hand over a woman like some sort of piece of property. Probably the second option.

"Fine. But I want a brokered meeting with Alpha Lathan," Chilton said. "I want this settled as quickly as possible."

Thaus could have grinned. A brokered meeting was the perfect front to make Chilton think the NALB was considering his request. Chilton would get his time to argue, and Thaus would rip the fucking contract to shreds anyway. Easy.

"Fine. Let me call the pack."

_N_o."

Lathan looked irritated enough to snarl at her. "Ariel, we have to be reasonable."

"I'm not doing it." She slammed the drawer closed and clutched her clipboard. Inventory. She needed to finish her inventory of the medical supply room, not listen to him try to justify the possibility of _this_. How could he even ask such a thing of her?

"It's just a meeting," he said, almost growling his frustrations.

But Ariel was not about to be swayed. "Then I don't need to be there."

"It's about your future."

"My future is here, in this pack, with my patients and my friends. Not mated to some Alpha with a ratty old contract who thinks I'm something he can claim as his own."

"Ariel." Lathan reached for her, a simple move that most people would have accepted as normal. Not Ariel. She stumbled back to avoid his touch, nearly crashing into the cabinets behind her. She hadn't flinched that hard in months, not around him, but this… This was different. This was life-or-death for her.

Lathan retreated, giving her the space he must have known she needed to calm a bit before he tried again. Not that she cared to listen to more of his nonsense. "I want you in the meeting. We've called in the NALB to broker these discussions since the Glaxious Alpha refuses to back down. They're here to assist on your behalf."

Bullshit. "Assist with what? Auctioning me off?"

"Never." Lathan's growl was a testament to the belief he held in the ruling party of shifters in North America, but that meant little to Ariel. She knew exactly how much went on without the NALB's knowledge, had been exposed to how dark some of the shadows in the shifter communities were, and she refused to be pushed back into them.

"He only wants me because I'm an Omega." Ariel shook her head, the weight of disappointment heavy on her shoulders. "If I'd never come to your pack, this wouldn't be happening."

"If you'd never come to our pack, you'd be dead by now." Lathan crept closer, giving her time to refuse him if she chose to. Pushing in a gentler way. "You're a good friend and a gift to this pack, more because of your kindness and empathy than your Omega status. We are blessed to have you with us."

"Then don't make me go to Glaxious." Ariel hated how sad she sounded, how weak. She'd promised herself she'd never be a victim again, but that's how she felt. Out of control of her own destiny. Unable to escape the coming tide of darkness. Helpless. "I do not want you to let him win this."

"I won't." He stepped closer, closing the gap. Leaving barely a breath of space between them as he stared at her with more fire in his eyes than she'd ever seen there. "I promise. If it comes to that, we will find a way to get you out of here."

And there it was. A harsh truth she would have preferred not to know. No matter how comfortable she felt with the Kwauhl, she wasn't a pack member. She was an outlier who could go back to a life on the road if she needed to. At least in Lathan's mind.

She edged around him, heading for the room she used to examine patients. "I don't want to run again."

"Sometimes running is what keeps us able to fight another day." Lathan smiled, as if he hadn't just ripped her world apart in a few small sentences. "I would never force you into something you didn't want, but you need to be at the meeting. If the NALB sees that you are adamantly opposed, they'll have to take our side."

My side, she thought. There was no *our* in this situation. "Fine, but don't expect me to be nice to these jackasses."

"I never expect what I know you can't give," he said, his joke falling flat. Whether he felt the tension, the pulling away Ariel had already begun, or something else, she couldn't be sure. But his next statement was far less friendly and much more stern. "One hour at the meeting room."

"Fine. I'll be there."

Ariel nearly sighed when he finally left her alone. Shaky and almost sick with fear, she finished writing up the order notes for the supplies needed, logged the vendors where everything could be purchased, and shut off the lights. She took one last look around the place she'd devoted so many hours of her life to, and then she left, probably closing the clinic doors for the final time. This wasn't home anymore. Perhaps it never had been.

But she wasn't completely heartbroken. Truth be told, she was far more angry than sad, which was a good thing because she had an arrogant Alpha to fight. She was ready to shift and take off through the woods for safety, but she'd show up for the meetings Lathan had called, if only because she needed to make sure her so-called pack understood why she'd soon be leaving them.

She didn't want to run again, but she'd have to. Whether from Chilton or from the group she'd never quite fit into, leaving appeared to be her only option.

An hour later, she hurried across pack property to the public house. The building was an old cafeteria from the first days when this land had been a campground for human families. The Kwauhl pack ran an adventure and exploring business, taking humans on group tours down the nearby rapids and up some of the mountains. It was good work, easy for the wolves, and made them all a good living.

But on that day, the campground seemed dim. Shadowy. Warning her of what was coming, the something lurking close by that would try to steal her from the light she craved. Ariel quickened her step in response to the sense of dread building, ready to get this meeting and the resulting good-byes over with.

"Hey, pretty girl." A man stepped out of the shadows near the porch, looking all sorts of wrong. The physical embodiment of trouble. Just what she didn't need.

"We've been waiting for you," he said as he stalked closer.

But Ariel wasn't one to let an implied threat get under her skin. "Let me pass."

"I think we should talk first. Make sure you understand all the benefits of joining the Glaxious pack." He stepped closer, looking her up and down in a way that made her skin crawl. "You won't be stuck with Chilton every night, sugar. We know how to share."

"Maybe, but do you know how to bathe?" She waved her hand in front of her face while edging closer to her destination. "Because, seriously, you might want to learn."

The man growled a rough and totally predictable epitaph, something along the lines of bitch or cunt. Ariel wasn't sure of the exact words because she was too busy dodging his lunge for her. Quick and agile, she practically flew past him, heading for the supposed safety the public house represented. Legs pumping and heart racing, she closed the distance in barely seconds. Not far, just a few more yards, almost there—

Too late.

A hand on her shoulder sent her brain spiraling into something close to panic. Some deep, dark, instinctual place that shattered her human mind but called her wolf forward in the blink of an eye.

The male became every shifter, everyone from that place. The men who'd harassed and tortured, who'd cut and burned. The men who'd held her down and climbed on top of her. Who'd done their best to own every single inch of her, no matter how much she begged for freedom.

She wasn't going back there.

Five

As it should be. These second-class packs can't just do anything they want. Why, the progressive presidents are destroying the very fabric of being a shifter in..."

Thaus gritted his teeth and tuned out the blathering Alpha. Why couldn't the mission have involved ripping something apart with his claws, strategizing some way out of a deadly situation, or anything dealing with explosions? Those were his skills. Listening to some asshole prattle was not.

At least they were out of the Glaxious territory. Thaus had spent a long, dark night in the woods surrounding it in an effort to try to avoid Chilton and his crew, but it was more than them. More than the shifters housed there. Something lurked in the woods. Thaus had felt it, sensed it. He was completely outnumbered there, far beyond the eight pack members Chilton claimed to have. He wasn't going back without extra men.

The sense of being watched, being hunted, had left almost as soon as they'd crossed the invisible border, and Thaus was finding it much easier to focus on Chilton. Not that he wanted to.

Hopefully, this walking, talking pile of wasted flesh would shut up soon.

"And another thing…"

Probably not.

"When I was a pup, my Alpha would have…"

Being in an enclosed space with the four men from Glaxious ramped Thaus' inner wolf up into a near frenzy. The need to dominate, to lead, to not have wolves at his back was hard to shake off, especially after a night spent wary and watchful. The rest of the men all sat silent and stoic, and Chilton, while not at all silent, looked pleased as punch. Calm, even. He was either putting on one hell of a show or completely out of touch with his wolf.

Thaus chose the first option.

The only thing that stopped Chilton's monologue was the appearance of other shifters as they arrived at the Kwauhl packlands. The offending Alpha looked over the men with obvious interest, an almost covetous expression on his face. Something was very off about the Alpha shifter.

A man with long, braided black hair approached as the Glaxious team and Thaus exited the car. Thaus' wolf immediately sat up and took notice of the new energy in their midst. There was something calmly demanding about the shifter, something powerful but quiet. Now, he was a true Alpha. Chilton's presence grew dim around such a wolf.

"You must be Sathaus."

Thaus didn't blink at the use of his full name, though it was rare for anyone except Luc to use it.

"Alpha Lathan," Chilton spat before the man could reach them, confirming Thaus' assumption. The weaker man knew his place, and he hated it. "You do not greet me as a guest?"

"You've been here before, Alpha Chilton. I was more

concerned with the new visitor." The man looked Thaus up and down, an almost devious expression on his face. "Though you seem like the type of wolf who'd rather watch than interact. That, I can understand."

The two Alphas grabbed forearms, exchanging the traditional shifter greeting. There was a marked difference between the two in Thaus' mind. Chilton was thin and wiry, but not in the same way as Lathan. The Kwauhl Alpha looked fit, as if he worked in his wolf form often and could outrun any other creature out there. Any except maybe Thaus himself, who was taller and bulkier but faster than most people would have expected. Lathan also seemed comfortable in his skin, even walking around barefoot as some shifters did to keep themselves grounded to nature.

Thaus liked Lathan immediately.

Meanwhile, Chilton was Still. Fucking. Talking. "You can't go up against a binding document, no matter what newfangled ideas about shewolf rights you may have."

Thaus bit back his growl. It didn't matter what Chilton thought was about to happen; he wasn't walking out of this meeting with the shewolf or even the promise of a possibility of getting his hands on her. If Thaus couldn't convince Chilton that this Omega had the NALB backing to do as she pleased, he'd have two choices. Call in President Blasius for the final verbal smackdown—or fight. He preferred option two, even if he still didn't know the odds against him.

As the Alphas argued back and forth, most of it coming from Chilton, an unexpected scent wafted by. Something decidedly human caught on a breeze and working its way across the mountain. Something unexpected.

"What is this place?" Thaus asked, interrupting Chilton with more than a little bit of satisfaction at having done so. The man needed to learn his place, and it wasn't lording over Thaus in any way.

Lathan cocked his head, a small smile on his face. "This is Camp Kwauhl. It's a place where human families can come and rent a cabin in the woods to escape the noise and traffic of the city."

"Ridiculous nonsense," Chilton hissed. But Lathan just waved an arm, a motion that encompassed the mountains almost surrounding them.

"These foothills have been our home for centuries, long before the rush of humans moved west. And for a while, these hills were too remote for the majority of them to access. But roads and forestry opened paths that brought more people, which, in turn, led to more trouble for us. We were constantly running humans off our packlands. Finally, the Alpha at the time said we should invite them in and devise a way to make money from them. Camp Kwauhl was born." Latham's smile grew, a sense of pride emanating from him. "We've been here over a century now, leading humans on adventures they can't get anywhere else on the West Coast. Our wolf instincts keep them safer than if they were out here alone, and we get to make money doing something we enjoy. It's a win-win."

Huh. Thaus didn't think he could have been more impressed by Lathan. Especially when he glanced over to see Chilton scowling. He took an immense—albeit immature—joy in seeing that man pissed off. Well done, Lathan.

They moved their party into a large, simple wood building, with Thaus taking more notice of the structures and residents of the camp. Odd choice, running something for humans. The idea made his mind itch, made his wolf growl in an anxious sort of way. Or maybe it wasn't the humans he could sense farther into the hills.

"Where is the Omega?" Chilton asked as the door closed behind the last man, sounding far more demanding than he had a right to.

"Ariel is working at the clinic," Lathan said, not very successful at holding back his irritation. "She'll be here soon."

An Omega with an angel name...

Thaus nearly stumbled as his mind locked in on the idea of what could be coming. Ariel...angel of nature. An Omega with an angel name. After centuries upon centuries of being a pack solely of men, three of his Dire brothers had found mates in quick succession. Sariel, Armaita, and Charmeine... all angel names. And though he didn't believe in coincidence or that he'd ever find a mate of his own, the fact that this Omega—this woman he'd been sent to protect—carried an angel name was certainly... Something. It was something he wasn't prepared to give much thought to, though. Not yet.

Luckily, the arrogant Alpha wasn't one to give a man a chance to let his mind wander. Chilton must not have been happy with Lathan's response. He positively sneered at the other Alpha.

"How disrespectful."

Lathan suddenly looked ready to fight. "She's a physician and has patients who need her care."

"Her original Alpha should have never let her leave the pack for that education, and you shouldn't have coddled her into thinking such a thing was a good idea."

Thaus perked up. So she wasn't from this pack? That could leave things in a precarious state. Without a strong sense of pack and a good bond, Lathan could choose to stop fighting for her just to get Chilton off his back. He didn't seem like that sort of leader, but it was a possibility. Thaus already knew his brothers would claim her as pack if they needed to, though how he'd do that without outing himself as a Dire Wolf, he wasn't sure.

Dire Wolves were long thought extinct by his shifter cousins. Bigger, stronger, and faster than a regular wolf, Dires lived far longer and fought far harder than others. His pack had proven that time and time again, as Thaus would if necessary. But the fact that seven Dire Wolves remained walking the earth was to be kept a secret. Something hard to do if he had to shift to wolf form in front of anyone who might know the old legends. Chilton wouldn't, but Lathan...he might remember the tales. Thaus' kind came with a larger skull than normal wolves and spots along their haunches—ermine spots. That sort of thing was hard to hide.

Lathan didn't back down from Chilton, though. Not yet, at least. "We don't confine our women here, which is one of the reasons she has no interest in a mating to one of your men."

"We have an agreement that your pack would give a she-wolf to mine at my pleasure. Today is my pleasure."

Thaus wanted them to stop making so much noise, but he was caught in a web of something. A sense of energy moving closer. A sense of fate closing in. Something was coming. Something important.

"That contract is over two hundred years old, and she doesn't want to go," Lathan said, growling slightly. Completely in touch with his wolf and ready to shift if necessary.

But Chilton still wasn't backing down. "The agreement says nothing about wants."

There. The hair on the back of Thaus' neck stood up, and his eyes locked on the back door. Something was coming in fast. Something big and dangerous that made his wolf want to investigate. Something none of them was prepared for, least of all Thaus.

As the two Alphas continued their bickering, the door opened and a woman walked in. A beautiful, dark-haired woman with skin obviously warmed by the summer sun and eyes as deep and dark as any night sky. The crowd of shifters parted for her, moving in two waves as she stalked across the room. Intriguing, stunning, sensuous...

And pissed the fuck off.

"Alpha Chilton," she spat, her eyes practically glittering in her fury. "If one of your men tries to touch me again, I'll do more than claw his face off. Now, let's get down to the meeting. I'm not accepting a mating… With anyone."

She stood with her chin up, her hands on her hips, and her face set in a solid glare as she looked at each man in turn. But when she got to him, when those almost black eyes met his, Thaus didn't just see her. He felt her. Like a kick to the gut, she invaded every one of his senses and sent his mind spinning. One shewolf, one look, one connection he couldn't deny. An angel to balance the demon he'd always been.

Things just got a whole hell of a lot more complicated.

Things just got a hell of a lot more complicated.

Ariel stood locked in place, unable to move. Unable to breathe. Her mate. For so many years, she'd traveled alone, running from place to place to stay alive. And she was good at it. She'd made it through scrapes most women, let alone men, would have succumbed to. But then the kidnapping... and the torture...and the escape that still ate at a piece of her. She was stronger in a lot of ways from that experience but weaker, too. Her mate had arrived, and the very thought of him touching her, reaching for her in any way, made her want to scream.

She was too broken for a mate.

"It's about time," Chilton said, his eyes hard and dangerous as he looked her over. "Let's begin so we can get our girl back to my packlands."

The low growl that reverberated through the room definitely wasn't hers, though Ariel had a feeling it was *his*. Her mate. The huge, muscular, downright terrifying man across the room from her. Why would the fates give her someone so rough? So scary? So…mean-looking? Did they not understand her? Had they not seen all that had happened in the past few years? Had they forsaken her for some slight and left her with only the one choice—this hulking menace of a man?

"My shewolf rejects your claim," Lathan stated, his voice clear and direct.

"I have a contract with your pack, and as a member of your pack, she is subject to its legality."

"She is also a woman with autonomy. She rejects your claim, and therefore, your contract is null and void."

"Ludicrous." Chilton pointed to the other man, Ariel's mate. "You're here to enforce the contract. Say something."

The man didn't flinch, didn't even glance over the small crowd to look her way. "I'm here to moderate and act as an NALB liaison."

Damn. His voice was rough just like him. Sandpaper against her skin, but in a good way. The kind of pleasure-pain way that sent shock waves down her spine. Gruff and warm and…intriguing.

Chilton, meanwhile, had gone red in the face. "And the NALB honors contracts signed between packs."

"But the NALB has long believed no wolf should be held in any form of a mating relationship without their consent," her mate said, that roughened voice making her tremble.

"Preposterous!"

Ariel tried to concentrate on the discussion that followed—on Chilton and Lathan and talks of boundaries and treaties—but the man the fates had brought into her life wholly distracted her. Being so big, strong, and healthy, he obviously wasn't from the Glaxious pack, which was good. That had been her first thought when she'd seen him. All the possible ways to escape, to get out of that hellish scenario, had filtered through her mind within those first few seconds. Thank the stars she wouldn't need to act on any of them.

That didn't mean she was out of the danger zone, though. Chilton didn't seem like the type to have much respect for a mating bond. Of course, she had no idea if the man the fates had chosen respected it, either. From the sounds of it, the man worked for the NALB, but he certainly didn't look like some sort of corporate drone—following directions and reading over contracts with a fine-toothed comb. Not with the size of his arms, the width of his chest, or the calm confidence he exuded. The surety of a man who knew how to use his body as a weapon when needed. Not possible.

His eyes—so light, they almost glowed—caught hers for a single look, a moment of connection, and she nearly sighed. He scared the hell out of her, but the draw to be closer was there, too. The need to be near him. He had to feel the same because he wasn't standing still. No, the man was slowly, almost imperceptibly, inching closer. Unconsciously giving in to the attraction.

Ariel shuffled her feet, biting her lip even as she took one solid step in his direction. It was a small step, a few added inches, but it soothed something inside of her. A tic at the corner of her mate's lips was the only sign he gave that he noticed her movement. That he liked it. She fell hard for that tic.

"But we had a contract." Chilton's screeching voice snagged her attention. A true feat, considering.

"No," Lathan said. "You and a former Alpha had a contract. I don't sell off my packmates as if they were cattle."

"This contract stands as valid. You owe me a mateable shewolf, and I choose her." Chilton pointed at Ariel, throwing his arm up in a way that caused a flashback to a different cabin, a different forest, a different time. A much worse one.

Ariel flinched, unable to stop it even though she hated

herself for showing such weakness. Chilton's words were so hard, his intentions so wrong, she had trouble keeping calm with him near her. Meanwhile, her mate positively glowered at Chilton, looking ready to show his teeth and bring out his claws. Her wolf slunk into the shadows of her mind, hiding from the fight she could feel coming. This situation had been volatile before she'd formed a connection to this imposing man—it had turned positively explosive since.

As her Alpha argued, Ariel considered her options. No matter what the decision, no matter who won the contract fight, she wasn't going to the Glaxious pack. She loved the little pack she'd found, but Lathan had made it clear she wasn't quite as bonded to them as she'd thought. So it was time to run again. She was good at running. She'd run from the bastards who'd kidnapped her all those years ago. Had run the moment they'd turned their backs and assumed she was too broken to have any self-preservation left. She'd run long and hard to escape the hell they'd tried to throw her into. But running didn't solve everything. She still had nightmares of that place—the darkness, the cruelty of her captors, the tortures they inflicted.

The other Omegas.

She'd run the moment she'd had a chance and never looked back, but the thought of those other girls trapped in that hell ate at her. She'd wanted to take them with her, to save them, too. But when the opportunity struck, no one else had been willing to try. They were too worn-down, too battered to take such a risk. She'd run alone, found her own safety net in the Kwauhl pack for a time. And she would run again if Chilton tried to trap her. She refused to be stuck in another situation where she couldn't make her own decisions.

That meant with her new mate, as well.

While Chilton and Lathan argued politics and NALB

guidelines, her mate stood solid and sure. Watching the fight before him. Ariel was certain he was watching her as well. She could feel it deep in her bones, sense his attention even though his eyes were focused elsewhere. The man was acutely attuned to her, and her wolf couldn't decide if she should preen or cower at that.

"You will come with me," Chilton said, stealing Ariel's attention back from her mate. She nearly gasped at the look on his face, at the hatred in his eyes. He was angry. Furious, even. And an angry wolf shifter was a danger to be around. But a weak shifter was easy prey, and she could not show weakness.

"I'm not yours." Ariel locked her knees, prepared to fight if need be. Her mate was close, less than six feet away and slowly moving closer, but he said nothing. A move that left her wondering at what point he *would* step in...if ever.

While she was focused on her mate, Chilton moved as if preparing to grab her. Ariel recoiled on instinct, and her stomach dropped as she saw the victory in his eyes. A deep growl whispered through the room, the sound of a wolf warning another, though she couldn't tell where or whom it came from. It didn't matter anymore—Chilton was stalking her like prey, and she refused to let him touch her.

"Back off, Chilton," Lathan said, his growl joining the other. Not that the Glaxious Alpha paid him any mind.

"I already took care of the man you had outside," Ariel said, feigning bravado even though her insides were positively trembling with fright. "Do I need to break every member of your little pack?"

Without warning, Chilton jumped in front of her, so close she could feel the press of his chest against hers. So near, her mind scrambled into panic mode. She couldn't move, couldn't breathe, couldn't hear or see anything but him. Could barely think straight enough to keep from screaming.

Trapped, trapped, trapped.

"You'll be mine, Omega," Chilton whispered as the room exploded into a cacophony of angry animal sounds. "I'll have that ripe cunt of yours whether you like it or not."

Her whispered "no" did nothing to stop him. Shaking, sweating, frozen in place, Ariel wished hard for some sort of calm. Some sort of peace so she could wrap her head around a plan of what to do. A way to escape. So she could function. The world slowed, time stopping as Chilton reached for her again. As he raised his hand as if to run a finger down her cheek. Seconds turned to minutes and then to hours, her helplessness growing the entire time. She couldn't escape him, couldn't convince her body to back up no matter how loudly her brain screamed it. She was completely at his mercy.

Until she wasn't.

One second, the bastard Alpha was reaching for her, smirking as if he'd won the dispute. The next, her mate was there, blocking her from her attacker, grasping Chilton's wrist as if to push his arm away. His movements were fast, sharp, and completely aggressive. An animal in attack mode.

And Chilton was his target.

But he didn't push. Didn't try to redirect the arm or shove Chilton away. Nope. He did what any menace of a man would do.

He grasped that wrist hard, and he snapped it.

Seven

*F*uck and no.

Thaus had never been so enraged, never so ready to knock heads as he was watching that so-called Alpha reach for his mate. She stood frozen in place, seemingly terrified, those seconds probably never-ending to her. Thaus knew the look of a panic attack, and she was definitely lost in one. She needed him. And he would not fail her.

He stalked closer as quickly as he dared, calculating angles and speed, working his way along the perfect trajectory to move directly between the two. To block Chilton from penning in his mate who obviously didn't want to be touched. Thaus had been watching Ariel as the Alphas argued, inspecting her. She was lithe and muscular with the sort of shape that came from endurance more than strength. Perhaps a bit thin, which was probably why Chilton had underestimated her. That smaller body didn't make her appear weak. Not to him. Thaus looked past the height and shape, sought something deeper to her. And he found it in the overlapping scars on her arms, the obvious damage left by some sort of restraining device around her wrists. She wasn't small and helpless like Chilton probably assumed. The woman was a fighter, a survivor, but something had pushed her past her limits and left her open for Chilton to take advantage.

Not fucking happening.

As Chilton raised his hand to touch Ariel, as if to do more than scare and speak, Thaus' restraint shattered. He roared and jumped forward, landing directly between the two. He bumped into Ariel as he did so, but he had no choice. That bastard wasn't laying a single finger on her.

Thaus grabbed Chilton's wrist. A simple act, one he couldn't help but push further when he saw the gleam in the man's eyes and smelled the arousal on the air. Chilton was getting off on scaring Ariel, and that sent Thaus into a full rage. He squeezed harder, letting his strength take the place of the words he wanted to say…

Snapping the bones with an ease that even he noticed.

Breaking the man's wrist hadn't been in his immediate plans, but he didn't feel guilty about it. Not one damn bit.

"The woman said no." Thaus growled his words, taking far too much pleasure in the pained expression on the other man's face. Lesson taught…maybe.

"She's to belong to the Glaxious pack." Chilton whimpered, trying to growl through it as he cradled his now broken joint. Still fronting as if he were something bigger and badder than he really was. "I claim her as my own mate."

The sound that came from Thaus was one of pure hell-born fury, though he held himself in check. Ariel was scared enough, her energy all over the place from where she stood behind him. He couldn't push her emotions any further without risk.

So he crossed his arms, and he calmed his voice into

something deep and dark but without the growl. And he glared at the bastard Alpha before him. "Not happening."

"You have no right."

"I have the backing of the President of the NALB."

Chilton's eyes went wide, the look in them one of almost fanatic giddiness. Well, shit. That couldn't be good.

"Then I and the Glaxious pack secede from the NALB, effective immediately. I will slaughter this entire fucking pack if I need to. The Omega will be mine."

Bullshit. But if Chilton wanted to play his hand that way, who was Thaus to disagree? "If you're no longer an NALB member, then I no longer need to be on my best behavior."

Without warning, Thaus snarled and struck, throwing a punch that landed right on the man's sternum. Chilton's chest nearly caved at the force of the blow, and his body flew across the room before slamming into the opposite wall. But Thaus wasn't finished yet. Not by a long shot. He stalked the fallen shifter, kicking errant limbs aside so he could crouch close enough for the injured Alpha to hear him. Looming over Chilton, really.

"She says no. She also has a name that isn't The Omega. You don't get to force her to do anything. Ever."

Chilton coughed a pained laugh. "I *will* have her."

Thaus wanted to kill the arrogant fucker for daring to threaten his mate, but the room had gone oddly silent. He took the chance on glancing behind him and immediately knew he'd gone too far for this audience. The Kwauhl pack stood staring at him as if he were the monster. Especially Ariel. His mate looked pale as she trembled with her Alpha at her shoulder. Thaus recognized the fear in her eyes, the apprehension that someone else was going to overpower her. He saw her anguish, and he hated it.

"What do you want?" Thaus asked, staring right at her, not letting her escape his attention for a second. "You have the control here, Ariel. You pick your future, and I'll make sure you get it."

Ariel stared at him, those deep, dark eyes locked right on his. The shock on her face, the idea that she was obviously taken aback by his words, grated on him even more. She didn't understand him yet, didn't know how much he'd do to make sure she was happy. She thought he'd make the demands for her, as if she'd never be heard with him around. He could see it, feel it, and that doubt crushed a little piece inside of him.

But his mate was just as strong as he thought, and that meant she took risks. The woman glanced at Chilton then back to Thaus, doubt gone, fear tucked back in place behind the warrior mask she wore. Ariel licked her lips as if preparing for a speech, and apparently, she was.

"I secede from the Kwauhl pack. I'm no longer a member, and therefore, not subject to any contracts in regards to the Glaxious pack."

Thaus nodded once, proud of her for taking advantage of that loophole. It wouldn't stop Chilton, but it made his access to her shrink to almost nothing.

The Alpha beside Ariel looked heartbroken, something that added fuel to the fire of Thaus' jealousy, but Lathan still didn't reach for her. Didn't try to touch her. He knew Ariel, definitely better than Thaus did. He knew her and hadn't been able to break through her walls. Thaus vowed to try, to follow her and keep her safe until she'd let him in. To protect her and do his best to understand her. He'd do better than some random Alpha, that was for sure.

Chilton's ragged cough and the scrabble of him getting to his feet stole Thaus' attention once more. The little man stood...sort of. More like hunched, unable to stand straight.

"I should kill you with my bare hands," Chilton said, his voice raspy and weak.

Thaus, meanwhile, felt just fine and dandy. "Try."

Chilton spat on the floor and snarled but headed toward the exit. Good thing, too, because Thaus would have been just fine killing the bastard had he tried to go near Ariel again.

"I'll be back, and I'll have my full pack with me. Don't bother running, girl. We know these mountains better than anyone and will track you down."

Thaus gritted his teeth, refusing to take the bait and chase the arrogant fucker. Because that's what Chilton wanted. He wanted Thaus so worried about *him* that he forgot about the men he'd brought. The ones who circled the building they were in, anxious and ready to take what wasn't theirs. What never would be. So Thaus kept his cool and waited the fuckers out, but once the Glaxious pack contingent had driven away, all bets were off.

"Close the camp," he ordered Alpha Lathan. "The humans need to leave the valley."

"Our last camper of the week left a few hours ago. We evacuated as soon as Alpha Chilton called this meeting."

"Good move. Now get your pack out of here."

Lathan looked positively insulted. "We can handle Glaxious."

"No, you can't." Thaus closed his eyes and let his senses spread, searching out energy and shadows. Using his connection to his Dires to help build a plan in his mind. His team was too far away to help, but he'd call them in as soon as he could. He'd need backup.

Lathan seemed annoyed as he tried again. "Cleaner Sathaus—"

"It's Thaus, and I'm not just a Cleaner. I deal with bastards like Chilton all the time. He's embarrassed and slighted, and he won't settle for anything less than annihilation."

"Our pack is larger."

"Wrong, his is. He has shifters in the woods, tucked

away and waiting for something. I couldn't get a good enough sense to know how many, but it's more than eight. My guess is, a lot more. Get your pack out of here because they'll all be coming for you, and I can't be your savior." Thaus met Ariel's worried gaze, making sure he infused his words with as much strength and honesty as he could. "She is my priority."

His mate didn't flinch, didn't look away either. The tension between them grew, the private bond forming in that very public space. Thaus had to stop it, had to turn away. Had to break the pull before he did something she wouldn't welcome.

"Go east," he told Lathan. "All of you—don't run, either. Drive. Head for Chicago and Merriweather Fields. When you get there, tell them Thaus sent you for protection. I'll be in touch when Glaxious is taken out."

The Alpha still didn't get it, though. "We can fight."

Thaus growled and stepped right into Lathan's space, his voice harsh. "His pack is larger by at least double— and five times as ruthless as yours. They'll fight hard and dirty in ways you'd never even imagine. They are feral, their wolves wild from the lack of true leadership, too sick of being under a weak Alpha's thumb. The second Chilton lets them get their wolf on to come after you, they'll be out for more than just blood. You won't win, and I don't trust Chilton not to slaughter all of you just to get back at Ariel."

Lathan took a good look around the room, eyeing each shifter. Everyone…except Ariel. "Can the NALB help us? This pack is important to the area."

Thaus tucked his irritation away. His Dire brothers would welcome Ariel into their pack, more than this guy ever could. "They will. But they're not close enough to reach you in time. Go to them. I'll call ahead and have the president send the Feral Breed out to escort you as much of the way as they can."

"And you think you can take on Glaxious?" Ariel asked. She doubted him, doubted his strength and strategy. A fact that didn't sit well with him.

But he'd prove himself to her. "I know I can, if we can get to a safe house before them."

"We don't want to leave forever," one of the other pack members said, eyeing Thaus and Lathan both.

"You won't have to," Thaus replied, taking the lead away from the Alpha. "The Glaxious have broken one of the very covenants of Blasius Zenne's presidency and a cornerstone of NALB regulations. Chilton won't be allowed to live."

The Alpha's brow furrowed. "What covenant did they break?"

"He's threatened an Omega." Thaus paused for a moment, giving himself time to take a breath. To meet his mate's eyes. To prepare for the words he needed to say. "He and his pack have assaulted a mated Omega."

"But Ariel's not mate…" Lathan trailed off, looking from Ariel to Thaus and back. Figuring out the connection without assistance. The room went silent, the rest of his pack watching and waiting. Anticipating. And looking to their leader to tell them what the situation was.

"Shit," Lathan hissed.

Yeah, that about summed it up.

Eight

*A*riel felt trapped between two hells inside her own mind. Her mate, Thaus, stood strong and ready to protect her, ready to claim her as his. He'd vocalized their bond, made it something real and weighted. And she…well, she sort of wanted to accept that. Sure, he was big and scary and she hadn't been intimate in any way with another person since she'd escaped her kidnappers, but the mating bond between them had suddenly become a physical, burning thing. Something deep and right and wrapped around her so damn tight, she didn't know if she could breathe through it. If she could even find her voice to tell him, yes, she was his, that she felt it, too. That she wanted it.

But that damaged, broken part of her resisted all her efforts to scrape out a place for herself, and that cage of hurt and fear left her mute.

"Shit," Lathan hissed, looking at her with eyes filled with concern. Her answering growl didn't seem to ease his discomfort. Too bad for him. She was pissed—at him, at herself, at the situation. And she was going to make sure they all knew it.

"Yeah." Thaus seemed surprised to hear her soft rumble, but she simply shrugged. He shook his head with a small smile before pulling a phone from his pocket. "We need to go, Ariel."

But her Alpha knew her, knew her fears and limitations. And he obviously felt a need to protect her, even from her own mate. "What are your plans? You can't just drag the Omega off the mountain."

"I'm not dragging *Ariel* anywhere." Thaus' fingers flew over the screen even as his eyes met hers, the stress he placed on her given name not lost on her. "I'm asking her to go north with me. I have a safe house there in the perfect spot to defend, way more advantageous than the valley we're in now. I'll call my team, and we'll eliminate the threat."

Lathan didn't look convinced. "The mountains get more treacherous north of here."

"Exactly." Thaus repocketed his phone, still watching Ariel. Still speaking to the Alpha as if he somehow mattered. "It'll take my team a day or two to get here. If we're lucky, the Glaxious will think Ariel went with your pack on the road. That mistake should give us time to hole up and get backup in place. But it needs to be somewhere fortified and protected. Which means north. I know those woods and that mountainside better than even Chilton ever could. I'll keep her safe."

His words were to Lathan, but the meaning was for her, the direct honesty a subtle reminder of the mating bond wrapping them tighter together. As was the look of sincerity in his eyes.

"And when your team gets there?" Lathan asked, eyeing Thaus in a way that made Ariel bristle. He knew her secrets, knew more about her past than the rest of his pack. And he knew how hard it would be for her to handle a houseful of strangers. Especially if they were the size of her mate.

Thaus, on the other hand, had no clue why Lathan questioned him. "My team and I will take out Chilton, break up the Glaxious pack, deal with whoever is lurking in the woods around their land, and remove the threat to Ariel."

"And you think it's going to be as simple as that," Lathan said with a disbelieving huff, earning him another low growl from her. Ariel's wolf apparently had no trouble finding her voice, either.

Thaus must have heard the rumble, though it was hard to tell. Just a small lift to one side of his mouth gave him away. Bigger than the tic she'd fallen for already, this was more like a smile trying to escape. Ariel would have liked to see such a man smile.

"None of this is simple," Thaus said, back to being Mr. Serious. "But it's necessary for Ariel's protection, and something my team is better equipped to handle."

"And a new mate during all of this? Can you handle that as well?"

Ariel darted a look to Lathan then back to Thaus, seeking some sort of reaction from her new mate. Something more than a tic or a smile.

What she got was a chilling look shot at her once-Alpha and a strong statement she had no trouble believing.

"I can handle whatever I must to keep her safe. That's my primary goal in all of this—save Ariel."

Lathan watched Thaus, sizing him up, before turning to her once more. "Ariel? You don't have to leave us if you don't want to. I know I talked to you about running, but we can bring you with us instead of just pretending to. The pack will do their best to protect you."

Every eye turned her way, every wolf waiting for an answer. But it was Thaus who held her attention. The man she couldn't look away from. The man she felt certain she'd be safe with. It was Thaus, in all his hulky, scary glory, who pushed her to finally find her voice.

"I'm going with him."

Thaus nodded once, in motion as soon as she voiced her opinion. "We should leave, then."

Ariel gave Lathan a sort-of smile. The most she could muster at that moment considering all she'd been through and all she knew was coming for her. "Make sure the pack is safe. We'll be fine."

"Of course, you will. And we'll be here once they get rid of Chilton." Lathan held out his hand, looking for some sort of trust but giving her the opportunity to refuse him. "Be careful."

"You, too," she said. Ariel ran a single fingertip along the length of his hand—which was about all she could handle at the moment—before heading toward Thaus. Toward her mate.

Toward a future she had no idea how to deal with.

Thaus led her outside without another word, not touching, but directing her with his body language and closeness. Ariel had regained a bit of confidence while in the familiar meeting room, but out there, alone on the mountain with a man she was oddly aroused by and terrified of all at once, she had trouble focusing. She practically trembled as he directed her into the woods.

"Are you ready?" he asked, his voice soft and almost soothing.

Ariel took a deep breath, digging deep for the shifter who'd fought her way out of a prison. Who'd almost ripped her own hands off to escape the bonds a group of men had tried to hold her with. The beast within who had kept her alive when she'd truly thought there was no hope for survival. That was the person she needed to be, even if it was only to voice her biggest fear.

"I'm afraid of you."

Something about Thaus gentled, whether it was the energy around him or simply the way he held himself. Ariel saying those four words suddenly made the man appear smaller and less threatening.

"I know." The calm, soothing sound of his voice gave Ariel another boost of confidence.

"I'm not comfortable around…people. And I'm not going to be jumping into bed with you just because we're mated."

"I never assumed."

"I don't like when things are forced on me."

Thaus cocked his head, his brow pulling down. "You think I would take something you weren't ready to give?"

There was a pain in his voice, a disbelief that ate at her. Had she…insulted him? "I don't know."

Thaus stepped in front of her, still not touching. Crowding her, though. Putting himself in her space and making her look up at him. "Yes, you do. Dig deep, mate. You should be able to feel my sincerity through the bond. It's new and just building strength, but it's there. Feel it."

Ariel stared into the ice-blue eyes imploring her to search for something she'd never known existed, trying hard to sense what she needed. To find some sort of safe ground inside of herself. Instead, all she found were fear and doubt.

"I don't feel it."

"Then I'll make you this vow," Thaus said, taking a step back and giving her room to breathe. "I won't attempt a single touch until you trust me."

"That might never happen."

"Then we'll be old and gray together without ever knowing the feel of the other's skin."

Ariel shivered at the growl in his voice, the underlying sensuality of it, struggling to resist the draw to touch him. Feel him. Taste him.

"I don't like this desire in me," she whispered. "I don't like being out of control."

"That's what I want you to understand, sweet mate. You are totally and wholly in control when it comes to us. Except for where we need to go." Thaus turned and pointed, drawing Ariel's attention. "There's a safe house north of here. It's a good twelve-hour run as wolves, but it's the most defendable place I can think of. Do you think you can handle the trek?"

"I'm stronger than I look."

His eyes slid to the scars on her wrists. The ones she'd given herself in her efforts to escape the chains. The ones that had taken weeks to heal and still ached when the weather turned cold and damp.

"You look mighty strong to me." Thaus stripped off his shirt and tucked it into a small pouch with an odd sort of strap looped over it. His pants went next, an action Ariel couldn't help but watch.

"We need to shift." He handed her the pouch. "There's a minimal amount of clothing at the safe house, so you might want to undress and put your stuff in here. I'll carry it."

She bit her lip, shifting from one foot to another, suddenly far more shy than she'd ever thought possible. Naked…in front of her new mate…while he was naked? That was a recipe for disaster.

"Will you—"

Without waiting for her question, Thaus shifted to his wolf and moved off between some trees. She barely saw him, only caught a glimpse, really, but it was enough to send a shiver of shock through her. Big, dark, with a large skull and a predator's jaw, the beast was something out of the storybooks. A legend, really.

But it was the spots along his spine and hips that screamed his truth.

Ermine spots.

The calling card of a breed of wolves long thought extinct but that she'd studied extensively during her school days.

As impossible as it seemed, she was mated to a Dire Wolf.

Nine

haus had been right about the endurance aspect of his mate's form. Ariel was a good runner, strong and sure, with a speed that almost matched his own. Without pushing herself too hard, the shewolf kept up with him as they raced through the woods, Thaus leading by barely more than a body length or so at any given time.

The long run gave the Dire plenty of time to surreptitiously investigate his new mate. She matched the look of the Mexican wolves from farther south with her deep, dark red fur. Much like honorary Dire member Angelita, the ward Bez and his mate Sariel looked over. Two women brought into the Dire world, both Mexican reds, both Omegas, both with angel names... If Thaus believed in coincidences, that'd be one hell of a doozy. But Charmeine and Armaita weren't red, so maybe he was just reaching for threads where there were none.

The phone inside the wolf pouch Thaus carried kept vibrating as the two ran. He knew who was calling—his Dire brothers, setting up the mission to come to his aide against the Glaxious pack. He knew it, and he sort of resented them. It didn't matter that Ariel would be safer with them close by; he secretly wanted them to stay away. He needed time with his mate, needed to get to know her, needed to understand the walls she'd built around herself and begin the arduous task of breaking them down.

He needed time with her, but time was a luxury he couldn't afford. Not with Alpha Chilton probably close behind him. The Glaxious pack would have to track by scent, which would slow them down considerably, especially as Thaus had led Ariel through as many streams and rivers as he could in an attempt to hide their trail. But eventually, the pack would come. Thaus wasn't stupid enough to think there was any way around that, which meant he needed his brothers with him. No Dire fought alone if they didn't want to, and the last thing he wanted was to go lone wolf when the stakes were as high as they were. He wouldn't risk Ariel.

When they finally reached the cabin after the long journey, Thaus shifted first. The pain in his shoulder burned throughout his body, and his shift felt less than perfect, but he couldn't concentrate on any of that. The safe house suddenly seemed ominous, and though he'd only just been there a couple of days before, had restocked it himself, and knew how defendable the building was, he worried he was making the wrong choice in where to plant his flag and defend.

"Ariel." He knelt in front of the small wolf, placing the pouch in his lap for a bit of modesty. Thaus had a feeling someone as walled off as his mate would not appreciate his cock waving in her face. The little wolf sat on her haunches and waited, eyeing him hard but staying far enough away so that Thaus couldn't have reached her. Not that he would have tried.

"This is my cabin, and I know how easy it is to defend and what weapons are inside." Thaus closed his eyes for a moment and took a deep breath, a feeling akin to fear building within him as he thought about the coming fight. About his brothers not making it in time. "I've got backup coming and I'm ready for this fight, but if anything happens, if the Glaxious pack comes and you ever feel as if this place and my plan aren't enough, run north."

Her tiny whimper tore at his heart and caused his protective instincts to surge. Fuck, he wanted to wrap his arms around her and let her feel his strength. Let her sink into it so she could understand how willing he was to fight for her. How dedicated he was to making sure she would get out of this situation.

"My pack leader is in Alaska. If anything happens to me, he'll know. And because we're—" a pause, almost unintentional but still there "—mated, because of our bond, he'll find you. He feels us all."

Ariel tilted her head, looking almost like a caricature of a wolf asking a question. One Thaus understood.

"You never have to fear me or my brothers. You will always be pack to us, whether you accept me as your mate or not. And you will always be safe with them." He took a deep breath, ready to lay out his secrets. The ones he'd been keeping for hundreds upon hundreds of years. "Ariel, did you notice the spots on my wolf's haunches? The size of his head?"

She chuffed, a small sound, but one Thaus took as agreement.

"My brothers all look similar. We're Dire Wolves, the last remaining seven in the world. We believe all Omegas are descended from our breed and are the female equivalent of our male Dire. If you see a wolf with spots and the same heavy bone structure as me, you can run to them. You can trust them. Those things mean they're a Dire, they're one of my brothers, and they'll do anything it takes to keep you safe."

She didn't react, though Thaus didn't expect her to. Scars like hers didn't fade quickly, but at least she knew. She had an idea of the Dire dedication to her. Hopefully, she'd never need to run for safety, but if she did, she knew what to look for.

Wanting to get his mate inside, he reached into the pouch and pulled out her dress. "I need to sweep the house. You can shift and put this back on. Just don't head into the woods." He paused, swallowing hard at the thought that crossed through his mind. The one that made him physically ache. "And please, don't run off. I'd have to chase you because of the attack coming, and…I think that would scare you. Let's get through the coming fight, then we can make decisions."

Thaus handed her the dress, which she took gently between her teeth. Her eyes never left his, and she refused to yield even an inch, it seemed. Strong, stubborn woman for sure. He could only hope she wasn't too stubborn to at least give him a chance to prove himself. He was no young pup, no hornball kid with more balls than brains. True, the pull to mate his female was a strong one, but he could control himself. Completely.

Needing to get things moving, he stood and headed inside, the gnawing fear of leaving her alone even for a minute tearing him apart. One quick sweep, and then he could be back at her side. He slid his cargo pants on the second he walked through the door, sniffing as he did. No new scents. No sign of intruders. Still, he kept an ear out for his mate as he moved deeper through the house. Every room investigated, every space cleared.

"Ariel," he called from the single bedroom at the back, knowing she'd hear him even through the walls. "It's clear. You can come in."

The wolf padded into the living room just as he came out from the hallway, her dress still in her mouth. The wolf, the dress…shit. Of course, she was too nervous to shift human alone outside. She'd obviously been prepared to escape if need be. Staying in her wolf form was the best way to do that.

"Sorry, I didn't think," he said as he ran a hand over his shorn head. "You can shift wherever you're comfortable. There's nothing to fear in here."

Except me, he thought. Because she did fear him, that much was obvious. A fact that caused him more pain than his bum shoulder.

Thaus moved to the windows of the living area—two of only four small ones in the entire house—making sure each was thrown open so the scents of the forest could carry in on the breeze. The battle would come to them, and scent was the easiest way for Thaus to know when it had arrived.

He turned around to head toward the rear of the house once more...

And almost died.

Ariel had shifted back to her human form.

And she had not yet gotten dressed.

His mate—his beautiful, luscious mate—stood in the middle of the living room, naked with her back to him, struggling to pull her dress over her head. Thaus tried to look away, but the mating pull was too strong. The need to devour her in any way he could too hard to resist. So he looked.

His eyes focused on all her soft bits first—her thighs, the swell of her hips, the curve of her stomach when she turned just slightly, the side of her breast he could just barely see under her arm. She was stunning and sensual in a way that nearly knocked him over. But that appreciation quickly turned to rage.

Scars.

Everywhere.

Claw marks, puncture wounds, long, straight lines that looked as if they were cut into her flesh with some sort of knife. They covered her body, creating what looked like a light-colored pattern across almost every inch of her skin.

Everywhere.

"What happened to you?"

His words were automatic. Unstoppable. And as soon as he said them, he wished he could pull them back. Ariel finally tugged the dress down, covering herself. Hiding those scars from his view. She almost seemed to shrink in on herself as if embarrassed.

"Like Glaxious, a group of shifters decided they wanted an Omega." She shrugged, her eyes staying locked on the floor instead of meeting his. "Or twelve."

Thaus' stomach dropped. The Omegas. The battle at Merriweather Fields, home of the NALB president, a mere three years before. He remembered it well. A pack with an Alpha set on harnessing the power of the Omega shewolf had kidnapped many of them from across the country and tried to forcibly breed them. He'd seen some of them at the final battle—the showdown when that Alpha tried to overthrow the president of the NALB. Tried to oust the Dires' current boss. The bastard had been defeated and the Omegas brought back home, but Thaus didn't remember Ariel from that group. He'd checked in every one, had carried most of them down to the hospital wing in the mansion after the fight was over. He would have remembered Ariel. He never would have left this mate once he found her.

"You weren't at the battle," he whispered, his voice rough and raw, his emotions much the same.

Ariel finally met his gaze, looking confused. "What battle?"

"Three years ago when the Alpha kidnapping the Omegas came to challenge President Blasius Zenne, you weren't there."

"No. I didn't even know there was a battle. I ran as soon as I figured out how to free myself." She held up her arms, putting her wrists together so the scars lined up just right. So he could see the circle from what had to be some sort of restraint, the flesh around it rough and jagged from teeth marks and the tears. Thaus was going to be sick.

Ariel, meanwhile, had lost a bit of the life about her. She spoke in a monotone with no expression on her pretty face. "Nearly had to chew my own hands off, but I got out of the chains. The other girls there…they weren't so lucky."

Thaus' head spun. So close. He'd been *so close* to finding her years ago. If they'd figured out what was going on sooner, if the Dires had been called in a little earlier, he might have been able to find her. He might have saved her from that hell.

But he was also so very proud. His mate had fought for herself, had escaped the enemy all on her own. Had… Why did she look so guilty?

"What is it?" he asked, taking a single step closer. Unable to hold himself back.

"The others. I've never forgiven myself." She turned her back to him, her arms coming up to hold herself. Something he wished he could do for her. "I tried to get them to come with me, but they wouldn't. Not a single one was willing to even try. I left them behind."

The pain in her voice, the anguish. He hated it. "We saved them."

Ariel spun, her long, dark hair flying out around her. "What?"

Thaus took another step, wishing with everything he had that he could wrap his arms around her, could comfort her. Knowing touching her was the last thing she wanted and hating every fucking wolf who'd ever touched her without care for that fact. "The battle at Merriweather, the challenge of President Blasius Zenne. The Alpha brought most of his Omegas he'd been—"

Thaus choked to a stop, unable to think about what the Alpha had been doing but knowing he had to.

"Fuck," he hissed, using every bit of his control to force his wolf back. The beast was filled with a fury the two had never experienced. Not even after being left for dead a time or two. Those bastards had touched his mate, hurt her, they'd—

"Breeding." He bit the word out, fighting to hold back the sick he could feel climbing up his esophagus. "They'd been forcibly breeding the Omegas. We saved most of the shewolves once the Alpha fell."

Ariel didn't miss a thing, it seemed. "Most?"

"There were...others. Before the fight." Thaus closed his eyes, remembering the cabin in North Dakota. The one with the six Omegas in it. The one they'd been sent to because of a pack in the Appalachian Mountains and a shewolf named Kalie. They'd almost lost some men that day, particularly the doc of the Feral Breed crew with them, but they'd done it. They'd knocked back the enemy and gained access to the cabin. He'd been the first one inside, and he'd never forget what he saw. Never forget what those bastards had dared to do to the Omegas they'd housed there.

Beds.

Chains.

Broken claws.

Dead eyes staring back at him.

No, that wasn't something a man ever forgot.

"But...you got them out? You saved them."

Thaus nodded, still feeling sick to his stomach. "Every one that could be saved."

Whether they wanted to be or not.

Ariel slowly dropped to the floor, her eyes unfocused. "I always hoped... I couldn't get them to go with me. I called the NALB as soon as I found a phone, but I didn't know exactly where I'd been, and I couldn't stick around to wait for them. I told them what I could, and then I ran as soon as I hung up the phone. And I just kept running."

"How long were you there?"

The way she hid her eyes from him, the flash of pain on her face as she turned away; that was all he needed to know. She'd been there long enough to have been raped. His wolf crashed against his mind at that knowledge, but he forced the animal back. This was not the time for fighting and growling. Not the time to show his strength and his fury. His mate was afraid and rightly so. They'd taken everything from her—her trust, her freedom, and her faith in the world around her. It wasn't his job to set the world ablaze to prove he would have protected her. It was his job to hold her together when she couldn't hold herself anymore.

And right then, he would have done anything to be able to do just that.

Instead, he said the only words he could think of. "I'm so sorry we didn't get to you in time."

Ariel shivered, a choked sob escaping from her pretty mouth. Thaus couldn't stand seeing her in so much pain. He reached for her, his movements slow and deliberate. Making sure she saw his hand coming closer. Giving her every opportunity to retreat if she wanted to. She watched him with wary eyes, looking at him as if he was some sort of predator. As if he'd hurt her like others had. As if he was a threat.

Ariel sat stock-still as his fingers brushed the back of her hand. The touch didn't last long, but it was a major step forward. The spark it sent up his arm, the way it caused Ariel's skin to flush, was more than he could have hoped for. And still, he knew better than to push for more. But before he could completely back away, she flinched, and his heart died a little bit.

"I'm sorry," he said, pulling away. Pissed at himself for pushing her too far.

Ariel shook her head, her shoulders hunching, her arms coming up to hang on to the opposite biceps as if hugging herself again. Or holding together the pieces left behind. "I just... I don't like to be touched."

"I understand." He inched back farther, giving her

space until the stiff set to her shoulders softened. "The mating haze will make that difficult on you."

"I know," she whispered, her voice shaking. "And I'm terrified."

A kick to the gut, but one he had to push away. That fear wasn't about him; not really. This was about Ariel and her past, and Thaus being uncomfortable or feeling pain at her truth wasn't something he needed to express. His mate deserved to feel safe in their relationship, to know she could tell him anything without him turning the attention to himself. He needed to be a good man to help her through this and a strong wolf to keep her safe.

Thaus ducked his head, capturing her gaze with his own. "I would never push you. I would never take from you."

But Ariel didn't look convinced. "You've said that."

"I mean it. Every time."

Quieter, softer…more honest than ever. "It's hard to take your words seriously."

"Well, you can. You're safe with me." He slowly rose to his feet, sensing she needed space. Hating that she did. "I need to secure the perimeter and get the other two windows open so I can scent anyone coming."

Ariel completely curled in on herself, hugging her knees to her chest and staring at the floor once again, refusing to meet his eyes. A move that might as well have been a direct hit to his heart. One hard to ignore. But he was strong, so he left her to her thoughts. Gave her the space she needed in that moment.

As he walked toward the back bedroom, though, her little voice broke the silence.

"Thaus?"

"Yeah?" He didn't turn around. Didn't risk scaring her by moving too fast or pinning her with his gaze.

"You really mean it? You won't…push me?"

He wished he could go back and kill those fucking bastards again. And again. Burn them alive, put them back together, and do it a second time. A third. Forever. "Not a single step. When it comes to you and me, we go at your pace."

"And if my pace is slower than a snail?"

He coughed a small laugh, risking a peek over his shoulder. "Then we enjoy the journey."

Ten

The mating imperative and resulting haze were no joking matter. As a doctor, Ariel had seen the effect on shifters a number of times. The blank stares, the flushed skin, the obvious desire pulsing between newly mated couples. She'd stupidly thought the fact that she hadn't sought out affection in years, had actually rejected it, would mean she wouldn't be as affected by the pounding need to join with her mate and claim each other with their bodies.

She was so bloody wrong.

Ariel paced the living room, unable to sit still ever since the conversation with Thaus had ended. Ever since he'd… touched her. And by the gods, she swore she could still feel that spark of electricity from the tips of his fingers. Every inch of her was suddenly attuned to Thaus' position. Every ounce of her attention dragging her thoughts back to him. One touch, one conversation, and that pull had shifted to a need, all because the man seemed…nice.

But *nice* completely underplayed Thaus. The word wasn't

strong enough, kind enough, rough enough, or soft enough. She didn't know if there *was* a word to describe such a person. He wasn't at all what she'd expected. Well, not around her, at least. He'd been brutal with Alpha Chilton but completely calm and reassuring with her. He seemed so large, so menacing, yet he'd been nothing but a gentleman. And the quiet way he simply moved about his life, staying close to her but never pushing her outside of her safe zone, was all the more intriguing.

Fear was a bitch with teeth, though. It held her back, stifling her need, creating a push-pull inside of her she didn't know how to conquer. Fear of touch, fear of being overpowered again, fear of losing control, fear of what was coming for both of them. Ariel had been living in a virtual bubble of assumed safety since she'd joined the Kwauhl pack, hiding away in the woods and avoiding anything scarier than the occasional raccoon in the trees outside her cabin. Now, she was on the run, chased by the Glaxious pack, and mated to a man who looked as if he could destroy half the world without even trying.

Bubble officially burst.

"Can you shoot?" Thaus asked, bringing Ariel to a stumbling stop in the middle of the room.

"What?"

Thaus, knife in hand from where he was prepping something to cook in the open kitchen, cocked his head. Those light eyes locked on hers, and she was gone. The heat that look sent flying through her veins was delicious and terrifying all at once. There was no avoiding it.

"I asked if you can shoot."

"You mean guns?"

An almost-smile appeared. "Yeah."

"Sort of. I'm no Annie Oakley, but I know how to aim and pull the trigger."

Thaus nodded, dropping his gaze back to the cutting board. "Good. There are weapons at your disposal here. I'll make sure you have everything you need for when they come."

Mating imperative or not, the reality of their situation was not something to be ignored. "You really think Glaxious will hunt us down?"

"Yes, but we have a little time. My guess is they'll run after your pack for a bit before doubling back to track us."

"That won't take long."

"No, but it'll be enough for my brothers to get here." He nodded toward the counter stools. "Would you like to sit with me while I make lunch?"

The decision was harder than it should have been, mostly because the closer she came to the man, the more she felt the pull to join with him as mates do. But Ariel wanted to talk to him, wanted to be near that beastly man, so she agreed. She moved to the seat, noticing how he made sure to keep the counter between them. To give her space, she assumed. Something few people would have done.

"You're curious," Thaus said out of the blue. His simple statement took her by surprise.

"I am. How do you know that?"

"A sense, I guess." His shoulder lifted in some sort of lazy shrug as he turned to the stove to tend one of the pans. "I sometimes feel things, energies of sorts."

Ariel hadn't expected *that* confession. "Like emotions?"

Thaus cocked his head, still not looking at her. "Like… predictions. I know where my pack is, not because I have a tie to them the way my Alpha has a tie to us, but because I sense their actions."

"That has to be difficult. Carrying the weight of that responsibility."

"I never thought about it like that, but it can definitely be a pain in the ass." Thaus reached for a pan hanging from a rack in the air and hissed, flinching in what was obviously pain.

Ariel was up and moving before she could consider what it might mean when she reached him. "What's wrong?"

"Nothing." His growly, grumpy response almost made her laugh. Typical guy, it seemed.

But she'd been healing patients for too long to let an arrogant, macho man stand in her way. "I'm a doctor. Maybe I can help."

But he just shook his head and took a step away from her. Trying to escape. The stubborn jackass. "It's nothing, really."

Ariel bit her lip, watching him. Weighing her options. He'd been kind enough to give her space, to keep from pushing her to do anything she didn't want to. She couldn't now force herself on him just because she wanted to help him. What precedent would that set? How disrespectful to his kindness would that be?

When Thaus raised an eyebrow as if he felt her emotional turmoil, she sighed. "I'm not going to push you, but how am I supposed to trust you if you won't give me the same consideration?"

Thaus froze, staring at her with a blank expression that told her nothing of where his thoughts had gone. She refused to break that look, though. Refused to back down from him for a second. Alpha males tended to try to overpower those around them, and she wouldn't allow that. Not this time. Medical care was her life's work; it was something that had carried her through year after year of heartache. She could touch others to heal them so long as they kept their hands to themselves, and she wanted to help heal him. It was really the least she could do.

"Okay," Thaus said after a long pause. Without waiting for another response, he pulled his shirt over his head and turned, placing both hands flat on the countertop and showing her his back. His very broad, very muscular, very mating-haze-inducing bare back.

And his scars.

"What is that?" she asked, lifting up onto the balls of her feet to get a better look.

"Medical intervention." He turned, giving her the front view of the bullet hole that had probably shattered his entire shoulder joint. "My Dire brother, Levi, was sent on a mission to determine if humans were getting too close to a pack. He met his mate there, and all hell broke loose."

"How's that?" She wanted to touch the little rosebud scar, wanted to feel how rough it was under her fingers. Wanted to...but held herself back. That touch wouldn't be purely medical in nature.

"The guy behind the mess convinced humans to get involved, and they brought guns."

"Guns don't do that to us." Ariel took a step back, then another, and another. Escaping to the other side of the counter once more. Tucking her need away for another time.

If Thaus was upset at her retreat, he didn't show it. He simply turned back to the pots and pans on the stove to continue cooking, albeit without a shirt on. "The humans in question? A shifter had told them about the pack in the mountains. The men were hunting the shifters, thinking those wolves were demons or something. The one who'd told them, though, was the mastermind. He'd wanted the pack Omega, my Dire brother's new mate, and he'd set up one hell of a scheme to get her. Taste."

"What?"

"Taste this." He held up a spoon, twisting so she could reach it. "Please. I want to make sure you like it."

Her instincts to escape flared, but only for a moment. Instead of a raging inferno of panic and fear, that heat was nothing more than the lighting of a match. A brief shot of adrenaline that burned off faster than she'd thought possible.

As if he knew, as if he felt her reservations, Thaus retreated slightly. He brought the spoon to his own mouth, tasting the sauce first. Giving something to Ariel she hadn't known she'd needed.

Reassurance that she was safe.

On his second offer, Ariel let Thaus feed her a small spoonful, keeping her eyes on his. Refusing to allow her body to tremble. The sauce was delicious, something that almost surprised her. The man could cook.

"It's good. Hot."

"Good will work." He pulled the spoon back and licked the red sauce from the edge, that long, pink tongue throwing static into her brain. The bastard knew what he was doing, too. He practically smirked as he dropped the spoon into the sink, grabbed a new one from the drawer, and returned to his stirring. And storytelling. "So creeper-shifter had figured out some chemical that would make shifters sort of…pass out. Knock them unconscious."

Ariel sat back, still a little shaky from that taste. "That had to be quite the chemical compound."

"It was." He pulled a huge pot off the back and took it to the sink. "Did you ever try The Draught when it was being produced?"

"No."

"Hmm. Well, that's what your kidnappers were using to dull the mating bonds of the women they stole. Fucked up the investigation for months. And that's sort of the base these assholes used for the knockout drug." Steam rose as he dumped the contents of the pot into a strainer set in the sink basin. "Problem was, when I was shot, the bullet that he'd coated in the stuff lodged in my shoulder. Instead of an easy in and out, the bone grew over it, and that caused some issues."

"How long ago was this?"

"Two years, seven surgeries, and three doctors telling me there's nothing more to be done." He shrugged again, wincing when he had to lift the heavy pot out of the sink. "So I grit my teeth when I shift and do my best so no one sees it."

"And you ache when you use that shoulder too much."

"Sometimes, but I only let it show in my den."

Ariel looked around the space once more, eyeing the empty walls and bare windows. "This is your den?"

The look he shot her, the one of lust and heat and downright need, almost knocked her right off her stool. "Feels like it."

It took Ariel a long few moments to regain her thought process, to remember what they'd been discussing. The heat from that one look would burn long after this conversation was done.

"So why not seek more help for that shoulder?"

"Because I'm a Dire Wolf. I'm not even supposed to be alive. We keep our secret close to the vest on purpose, so I can't just go see any shifter doc. If they figure me out and happen to blab, my entire pack is screwed. Besides, your kind is a bit rare as it is."

"Shifter doctors? Yeah, we are."

He tossed a white hand towel over his shoulder and leaned against the opposite bank of cabinets. The picture of confidence and comfort. And still half naked. "What made you want to be a doctor?"

Quit staring at his abs. "I didn't...not really. My pack needed one. The town nearby needed one. So I went to school and fulfilled that need."

"That's it?"

"That's it. There was no big draw to help people or save the world. No altruistic feeling of being in service to my fellow shifters. There was a problem, and I fixed it. I wanted to stay close to my pack, to live as far from the city as I could, and being a doctor gave me the skills I needed to be able to interact with the human society around me without questions."

"Why didn't you go back after…" He trailed off, looking slightly uncomfortable, which explained exactly where his mind had gone. He wasn't the first man to know her story who had no idea how to address it.

"After I escaped the rape chambers?"

The fury in his eyes practically burned her skin, and the growl that escaped him felt like sandpaper for her ears. "Yeah."

Another shrug, another dismissal of something that she'd taken a long time to decide. "It wasn't safe there. They'd taken me from that place; I couldn't go back and give the bastards a second chance or risk the people I'd grown up with. So, when I escaped, I ran west. And here I am."

Her words hung heavy between them. A living force of lies and omissions. She could have gotten into far more about her experience—the smell of the men who'd stolen her sense of self, the nights she'd lain in bed covering her ears to keep from hearing the screams of the other girls, the pure terror of her race across the country and away from everything. She could have laid everything out in front of her and let him see every brutal secret. But she wasn't ready for that, and deep down, she didn't think Thaus was either. So she held back, kept her language casual and dismissive. And he allowed her that.

Thaus tossed the towel on the counter and grabbed two plates, giving her time to breathe again as he turned his back to her. "Where would you like to eat?"

Ariel took a single, deep breath before resettling into herself. This was okay. This would all be okay. She could handle the current level of friendship between them so long as he kept letting her hide when she needed to. And she had no doubt he'd do that.

"Here?" She motioned to the counter when he turned back around.

"Sounds good." He set the plates down, still keeping the counter between them. Ariel wasn't sure that was necessary anymore. At least, she hoped not.

"You can sit next to me." She nearly blushed when his eyebrows went up and his eyes shot to hers. "If you want to, I mean."

"And you're okay with that?"

"Snail's pace…not frozen, remember?"

He smiled and grabbed his plate. "Yeah, I sure do."

Before he came around the counter, he pulled his T-shirt back on. A travesty in Ariel's opinion, though she didn't voice it.

Sitting beside Thaus wasn't nearly as awkward as she'd assumed it would be. He kept a good space between them and didn't push her in any way. He was slow with his movements, warning her plenty before he reached for something anywhere near her. She liked it. She also hated it. She suddenly wanted him to sneak a touch in, to hold her hand or rub a finger along her cheek. She wanted for him to at least try. But she'd set the rules, and Thaus was a good enough man to follow them.

Damn him.

As they cleaned up, Ariel's mind wandered back to the meeting house. To the Thaus who'd stood silent and still, watching her. He was a vastly different shifter than the man before her.

"You don't talk much around other people, do you?"

"Hmm?" He glanced up from the sink where he was washing the pots and pans.

"I just mean, you're talking with me."

"You're my mate." Simple, precise, accurate...exactly what she expected.

Still, she blushed. "Right. But back at camp, you were all silent and intimidating."

"I was intimidating?"

"Yes. Total intimidator."

"Huh." He turned off the faucet and moved toward the windows, staring out into the dark night. "I don't need to fill space with sound, especially in crowds. I prefer to watch."

"So you're a voyeur."

The words were out of her mouth before Ariel actually thought them. Before she realized how sexually charged they could be.

Thaus growled low and deep, turning slowly, a heat in his eyes that made her tremble. "When this snail's journey is over and we reach our destination, you'll find out exactly how much I like to watch. Promise."

By the stars... "I have no idea how long it would take for me to..."

"Doesn't matter." He crept closer, telegraphing each move before he made it, giving her time to run. But she didn't. Wouldn't. She wanted something. Wanted it with a burning need she couldn't get under control. She just didn't know what *it* was yet.

When Thaus finally stopped right in front of her, he held out his hand. A simple, open palm displayed to her. No demands, just an offer she could choose to refuse or accept. Ariel stood and stared at his hand for what had to be minutes, noticing every line and wrinkle. Memorizing the shape.

"Your pace, Ariel."

She nodded, still staring at that hand. Slowly, she raised her own, hovering over his for a long moment before letting her fingertips trail along the warm skin of his palm. His growl deepened, but he didn't move. Didn't attempt to push things further. He let her lead him. Ariel stroked the length of him again, still with just the tips of her fingers. The heat of that touch burned, and the need that fire caused intensified. A simple touch of his hand, and she was lost. Shaking. Needful. But still not ready.

Eventually, she pulled away, smiling up at him. Knowing how hard standing still like that had to be on a mated male with instincts to claim. "Thank you for…being a snail with me."

He held her gaze, completely focused on nothing but her. Giving her no room for doubt as he whispered, "Anything for you."

Eleven

Thaus prowled the land around the cabin for hours after their late lunch, giving Ariel her space and trying to work off the tension in his body. He didn't go too far, though, always keeping close enough to see or hear what was going on. He couldn't stand the thought of leaving Ariel by herself, but he already recognized how much she wasn't ready for him. For anyone.

His entire world had flipped upside down from the moment he saw her; he could only imagine how she felt. The tremble in his mate's voice every time she spoke about their mating, the fear in her eyes—they drove him mad with rage. How dare someone hurt that shewolf? As much as he would have liked to have met her sooner, deep down he was glad she wasn't at the battle at Merriweather. He'd been brutal there, and in the resulting searches after the fact, completely owned by his animal instincts. All those women, those Omegas…all the babies those bastards had forced on them. His Ariel could have been one of them, was at one time. She could have seen him at his most violent. The thought was enough to make him sick.

Darkness had long since fallen when he came up over the rocky hill to the area directly in front of the cabin. He wanted to go inside, to see how Ariel was doing, and spend time simply in her presence, but the coming danger kept him moving. One more loop, and he'd give up. One more trek to make sure there were no new footprints or scents. One more—

"Anything?"

Thaus spun, snarling, his claws out and his hackles raised. But that soft voice eventually broke through his protectiveness. He knew that voice. Had been longing to hear it since he'd left his mate inside the cabin to come out on this perimeter run.

Ariel stood on the porch, looking into the darkness, bathed in the golden glow spreading out from the single light on in what had to be the living room. An angel in the flesh. A worried one.

"Thaus?"

His shift hurt more than he cared to admit, more than he was ready for, but he rushed it anyway. For her. Always for her.

"Sorry. I was...lost for a second." He stretched his fingers, waiting to approach until his claws retracted and he could stand up straight. Fuck, his shoulder was getting worse every day. "Nothing yet, Ariel. You should be in bed."

Bed. Shit, there was only one. A huge, soft thing he'd dragged up this mountain years ago. He could just imagine her golden skin on the white sheets, her long, dark hair fanning over the pillow.

Fuck, he could not be hard with her staring at him like that.

Ariel shrugged, clueless to the place his thoughts had gone and to the battle between him and his errant erection, looking decidedly uncomfortable, though. "I can't sleep. I keep thinking they're going to come blasting through the window or creep in through the door."

Thaus growled long and deep. "That won't happen. They won't get near you."

"You can't be sure."

"I can. Besides, I think we have a day or two until they decide to come up the mountain."

"Why do you say that?"

"Because that's the sort of decision a poorly trained leader would make. Once he figured out the ruse of the escaping pack, he'd wait until he had his troops ready for his next move, and then he'd attack."

Ariel was quiet for a long moment, still searching the dark for him. Still looking too fucking beautiful for him to know what to do with.

"What would you do?" she asked, her voice soft. The sound trembling in the night air.

Thaus couldn't stay away, not when his mate seemed so distressed. Not when she was obviously frightened. He inched closer, his steps slow and steady so as not to push her into flight mode. Stopping only once he reached the bottom porch step.

"I'd have already done it," he said as her eyes finally found his. "And I'd have won because surprise would have been on my side."

Ariel stared at him, her eyes wide. Even in the dark, he could see the slight flush to her cheeks. Smell the warm, summery scent coming off of her. The desire she refused to give in to. His mate had needs she wasn't addressing, needs his wolf would have given anything to fulfill. She wanted... and Thaus didn't know how to help her.

"Ariel?"

"I'm going to take a bath." Ariel disappeared inside before he could blink. Running. His mate was running from him in her own way, bottling up all the desire she felt and refusing to let it out. The sting of rejection hurt, but he couldn't let that slow him down. She would come around to him, and if not, he'd follow her like a lap dog to keep her safe. That was his purpose, his sole focus. And he'd do it well or die trying.

But there was still a job to do, missions to complete, battles to fight that had nothing to do with her. Shit, how the hell did his Dire brothers go out on missions knowing their mates were at home? Sure, Deus, the techie of the group, had fitted each house and business with ridiculous security, but that wouldn't be enough for his Ariel. What if she woke up afraid? What if she needed him close? He couldn't leave her holed up in some compound the way Bez left Sariel, and she didn't have a huge family watching out for her like Levi's Amy. Even Mammon's Charmeine wasn't in the same boat—she had a full pack of misfits around her with armed guards and a mob boss watching over them all. His Ariel would have to be left with her small pack, the ones who couldn't have protected her. The ones who seemed nice enough, but didn't have the fight in them to tear others apart if necessary.

Distracted, Thaus stomped into the cabin and locked the door behind him. A slab of wood wouldn't keep a shifter out if they truly wanted in, but it gave him a sense of rightness to engage the lock. A sense of security. The door didn't have to stop anything; it only needed to slow an intruder down enough for Thaus to realize someone was coming in.

Once done locking up, he moved from window to window, shutting and locking each one. Securing his den. Securing his mate.

As he stalked down the hall, though, something caught his attention. A scent on the air, a small sound he couldn't place. He inched quietly toward the closed bathroom door, knowing Ariel was in there. Sensing something coming from her that he'd never noticed before. Intrigued by that warm, honeyed scent.

"Mmmmmm."

He cocked his head at her moan; every ounce of his being homed in on her. Was she…? That sweet scent wafted over him again, and he nearly shook with need. His cock grew hard, swelling almost painfully in a matter of seconds. Aroused. His mate was aroused. Without him.

"Oh, Thaus…"

He nearly stumbled against the door. She'd moaned *his* name. His. That made him feel better and worse all at the same time. She didn't want him to touch her, but she was fantasizing about him. What the fuck was he supposed to do? Ignore her moans? Leave her to satisfy her needs alone? That wasn't his way. Would never be. If his mate needed release, he wanted to help her reach it. But she wouldn't let him close enough to satisfy her. Couldn't stand to have him touch her. He was completely at a loss.

Hell had come to his little cabin on the mountain, and it had come hard, hot, and wet.

"Ariel," he called after her next moan, one shaky hand braced on the door as if he could reach through and touch her. "Are you…okay?"

Her breaths came faster, the sound of water splashing growing louder. "I'm…fine."

"Ariel." He released a growl from deep within himself, purposefully dropping the register to a level that another wolf would instinctually know meant mating. She might not want his touch, but she obviously wanted him. So he threw caution to the wind and gave her what she wanted. "Are you touching that soft pussy, baby? Are you thinking of me while your fingers slide over your slick skin?"

She was silent for a long moment, the only sound her heavy breaths. He waited, prickles of energy running in rivulets along his skin. That silence carried weight; it pressed on him. Made it hard to breathe. But then his mate groaned, and he knew he had her. The sound was so soft, she had to be biting it back. A damn shame, really. One he needed to put an end to.

"Don't do that, baby. Let me hear you. I won't come in and I won't touch, but I can talk. I can let your wolf hear her mate."

"Oh, Thaus."

"That's a good girl." He settled against the wall, leaning toward the door so he could be as close to her as possible. "Are you touching yourself, Ariel?"

"Yes."

Oh hell, how his cock ached for her. "Good. That's good, baby. I want you to. I want you to drag your fingers over your pussy. I want you to rub a fingertip on that pretty little clit. Can you do that?"

Ariel went silent again, though the sound of splashing told him she was doing as he asked. He could just imagine her in that big, white tub. Hair all down over the edge, skin dewy and warm. Legs spread on the rolled edges for leverage. Fuck, he was going to come in his pants if he kept that up.

"Oh, yes," she cried, her heart rate building and the sound of small splashes growing louder.

Thaus closed his eyes and pressed the heel of his hand against his hard cock. This was going to be painful. Super fucking painful. "That's good, baby. Keep doing that. Run your finger over your clit and imagine it's my tongue. I want you to tease yourself with that hand. Want you to think it's my mouth on your flesh."

"Oh, fuck."

Yes. He could hear the desire in her voice, the need to finish. "You want me to fuck you, baby? Okay, then. We can do that too. Just use your other hand, baby. Bring your fingers to the opening of your sweet pussy."

"Thaus, I'm…I'm…"

"I know, Ariel. I can hear it. I can fucking smell it, baby. I'll get you there. I'll make you come so hard, you won't ever want for another's voice or touch. Just me. Me and you and every ounce of my focus on your sweet pussy as I push you right over the edge." He growled again, keeping the sound going, rubbing his palm over his cock in an almost unconscious move as his body reacted to her sounds. "Are you using both hands, Ariel? Are you fucking yourself with your fingers?"

"Yes," she said, her voice almost a sigh. Closer to a moan.

"Good. That's good, baby. I want you to keep rubbing that little clit while you slide a finger deep inside." Her groan nearly killed him, but he wasn't done yet. Not by a long shot. "That's my girl. Pump it in and out a few times. Get that finger good and wet. I know your pussy's creaming for me, baby. Tell me it is. Tell me how sloppy I make you."

"Yes, Thaus. I'm so wet…for you."

He'd never heard anything hotter than those words. "Good. That's so good, Ariel. Now add another finger. My cock is big, baby. It'd stretch you for sure. Got two? Add another. I want you stuffed. I want you imagining you're riding my big, thick cock right now. Imagine me underneath you, teasing your clit while you ride me. Because I would. I'd tease it good. You'd be dripping wet before you even mounted me because I'd spend an hour between your thighs. I can almost taste you already. Sweet and ripe, a true feast for a bastard like me. I'd lick every fucking inch of you. I'd slide my tongue inside your pussy and make you scream my name. And then, only then, when you were positively sopping and still trembling, would I pick you up and set you on my thick, hard cock. Only then would I thrust up into your swollen, soaked pussy."

"Thaus…" Ariel panted, the sound of water splashing against the sides of the tub louder and more rhythmic. She was close. Hell, so was he, and he still had his pants on.

"Fuck, I want to feel it. Want to know how tight your pussy will squeeze me when you're ready to come. I want to feel you milk my cock as you're screaming my name."

She gasped. "Thaus, I'm coming."

His snarl was unstoppable, his claws digging into the wood of the door as he lost some of his control. "That's it, baby. Come for me. Give me all that sweet release. I'd fuck you across the bed if you came on my cock. I'd never let up, keep teasing more from your little body. I'd fuck you until you screamed for all the right reasons."

And she did. She screamed his name, the sound turning to a groan as the air positively filled with the scent of her arousal. Thaus couldn't resist, thrusting his hand down his pants and grabbing his aching cock. The tip was slick with precome, the head swollen and sensitive. He wanted Ariel to be touching him, wanted to feel her walls tremble around him, but not yet. She wasn't ready, so he'd keep things to himself. And by things, he meant his cock.

He wrapped one big hand around his length and tugged, spitting out a hushed curse as he tugged on the foreskin. Fuck, that felt good. Not enough, not without his mate, but with her scent all around him and knowing she'd just come not ten feet away from him, it was borderline adequate.

As his mate's breathing slowed, Thaus groaned and worked his hand over his cock. Tugging and pulling and thrusting up, chasing his release just as Ariel had chased her own. When he was close, he unfastened his pants and pulled them over his hips, too anxious to take them off, too needy to give a lot of fucks about the mess he'd make.

Sliding his hand back to his cock, he stroked and rubbed and twisted and grunted with only thoughts of his Ariel on his mind. Only the feel of warm and wet and rough on his cock until he came in his own hand. Until he whispered his mate's name as he released with her image in his head.

"Shit," he hissed as he gave himself one final stroke, his cock too sensitive for much more yet. "You okay in there, baby?"

Ariel was quiet for a long moment. "Yeah. I'm...good."

Thaus sighed as he rubbed his wet hand on his shirt. She sounded nervous again. Afraid, maybe. But the padding of her feet across the tiled floor had him leaning closer, pressing his side against the door, wishing she'd open it so he could see her. But he knew she wouldn't. Sensed she wasn't ready yet.

"Thank you," she whispered, her voice so much closer than it had been.

He ran a finger over the wood, his heart aching and his body itching to touch her. "You're welcome, baby. I'll talk you through it anytime."

She chuckled. "You're dirty."

"I am."

"Someday..." She trailed off, but he knew. He understood exactly where her mind had gone.

"Someday will be amazing. But today wasn't half bad either."

"No, it really wasn't."

If there was ever a time to give her space, this was it. Thaus could feel it, could sense the tension growing within her. She needed time alone again, and he needed to get himself cleaned up.

"I need to patrol, baby," he said, the excuse coming easy and true to his lips. "You should try to get some sleep."

She sighed. "Yeah. I think I will."

One more pat to the door, one more moment of staring at that barrier and wishing he could just destroy it. "I'll be right outside. No one will get past me.

"I know that, Thaus. I don't know how, but I know that."

"Good. Now get some sleep."

It took every ounce of control he had to finally peel himself away from the door and head for the kitchen. After a quick wash-up at the sink, he headed outside. How he did it, how he walked out without his mate beside him, he'd never know because it was the absolute last thing he wanted.

Still, the night air felt good against his overheated skin. His human mind had started to settle, but his wolf reared the second they stepped outside. It sought control, pacing and on guard as it waited for a turn to rule the body they shared. Something other than a satisfied mate and a lonely hand job had the beast on edge, and that was bad news. Thaus stripped off his pants and shifted, wanting to feel the earth under his paws and let the spirit of the forest grow around him. Wanting to give himself to his wolf senses to determine why the energy was all sorts of wrong.

He padded through the trees, sniffing and letting his wolf see the night for what it was. Letting him sense whatever was out there. And there was something out there. Something dark and dangerous, moving closer. Coming for them. A sense of being surrounded, penned in. At risk.

With only thoughts of Ariel on his mind, Thaus raced back to the porch where he'd left his pants, shifting human in the middle of a step. Not even the ache of his shoulder could slow him down. His phone was in his hand within seconds, his fingers dialing just as quickly. He would *not* risk her for pride. He couldn't.

Phego picked up after just one ring. "S'up?"

"How many hours out?" Thaus asked, his words almost breathless.

"Still twelve or so. I've got Mammon with me."

That pulled Thaus up short. "He left Charmeine alone?"

"Barely. I thought he was going to toss her in the suitcase and drag her ass with us."

"Shut up, motherfuckers," Mammon yelled in the background.

Phego chuckled. "He made Bez come stay at the farm with her and the pack, which means Sariel is there as well. It's a big old party down in Texas right now."

Thaus grunted, understanding Bez's reasoning completely. "I may need you here sooner than twelve hours, and you'd better call Deus for backup."

"Situation?" Phego asked, suddenly all business.

Thaus sighed and ran a hand over his shorn head. "She's my mate."

"Holy shit." Phego mumbled something, as if covering the phone to speak to Mammon. The hollow sound of the device switching into speaker mode came next. Fuckers.

"What's going on, man?" Mammon asked, his voice a little tinny. "You think we can't handle the threat?"

Thaus growled, his irritation only growing. "I can handle anything. Normally. But this time…with her…"

"I hear you, and while I'm totally thrilled for you, I get where your fear is coming from," Mammon said, all joking tucked away at the thought of a mate in danger. "But what's the threat situation? Think logically for a second."

Thaus closed his eyes, letting the energy in the air wash over him. Feeling for the darkness he'd sensed earlier. And finding it. "They're coming for her now. I can feel them. I can't tell how soon or how many, though."

More mumbling, then Phego picked up the phone. "Mammon's calling Dante to see if there's a plane nearby we can jack. We're coming, man."

"Yeah. Perfect. Just…ping off my coordinates."

"Hey, I get that you're superconcerned, and congrats on the new mate, but this ain't our first rodeo. We'll get there."

"You'd better." Thaus hung up, not sure whether to feel relieved or not. He wasn't used to being so unbalanced. He'd been a decision-maker for a long time, but for this mission, he couldn't trust himself to do the right thing. His mind was clouded by thoughts of Ariel, by nightmares of her in danger. He needed his pack to keep him from making the wrong decision in the heat of the moment.

And he needed to arm his mate so she was ready for what was coming.

Twelve

The next morning, it took Ariel a good twenty minutes of pacing to get up the nerve to walk out of the bedroom. The one she'd stayed alone in all night, with the softest, biggest, most comfortable bed she'd ever slept in. Thaus' bed. She'd fallen asleep to the scent of him wrapped around her, and she'd slept hard. No tossing or turning as the night ran on. She'd slept like a log after the whole coming to the sound of his voice thing.

By the gods, just the thought made her blush.

Her orgasm had been amazing, her sleep incredible, but by the light of the morning, she worried about what Thaus thought of everything. Would he expect her to be ready for more? *Was* she ready for more? She didn't think so, but she also had never thought she'd get off with a man she'd only just met talking dirty to her through a closed door.

She really wished she could hide for the day.

But a threat was out there, and Thaus had said his team would be arriving. Ariel assumed that meant today, so it was time to grow up and face the music. With her cheeks and ears positively on fire.

"Morning," Thaus said as she walked into the kitchen. He didn't turn around from the stove, though. Ariel was oddly disappointed in that.

"Good morning," she said softly. Not sure where to go or what to do. "Uh, can I help with something?"

"Got it all covered."

And he did. She stood to one side and watched as he cooked eggs and sausages. How one got eggs out of frozen or pantry food, she wasn't sure, but Thaus obviously did because that seemed to be what was for breakfast. The smell of food cooking almost made her mouth water, but it was the sight of his long, hard arms bulging and straightening that kept her attention rapt. Every muscle, every curve of flesh, was more intriguing than the last. She wanted to feel them, to place her hand over all that strength and touch that power. She wanted to know what it was like to be wrapped in arms like those, to be held by them, protected by them. A thought that startled her with its intensity.

Thaus coughed, though, and Ariel snapped back to herself. She'd taken a few steps closer, had even begun to edge around the island. She also had just about soaked her panties. Of course. Which must have been why Thaus coughed. He could smell how aroused she'd become. She hadn't thought her skin could burn any hotter than when she'd walked out of the bedroom. She'd been wrong.

Ears on fire, Ariel moved across the kitchen area and grabbed a towel. She needed to keep busy, that was all. To stay distracted from that man's body, his muscles, the easy sensuality with which he seemed to complete every task. She needed to do anything other than stare at him. So she wiped down the counter where they'd sit with more vigor than probably needed. Once completed, she headed off to find the utensils and plates to set their places.

"Almost done?" Ariel asked as she walked past Thaus, who'd just turned the burners off. She must not have been loud enough, though, because he jerked and spun.

And he grabbed her bicep.

For one tiny moment, she relished that touch. She'd craved it so much that to have it, to feel him, was a moment of bliss she couldn't deny. But the agony of fear, the building of panic, wasn't ready to pull its claws from her psyche just yet. Thaus must have known, must have seen the switch flip inside of her. He let her go quickly, released her to stand on her own even though she'd been leaning into his touch. Threw his hand up and gave her the room he must have assumed she needed to calm herself.

But, oh, how he was wrong.

There was no more calm to be had. Not with him so close. He made her dizzy with desire, made her body clench for things she wasn't ready for yet. He made her need. That was why it had to have been an accidental move on her part. A clumsy, half-stumbled, single muscle twitch that knocked her off-balance and sent her arm forward. That caused her to brush her mate's hand with her fingertips. That made her grasp his arm with one hand for support.

Had to be.

Thaus stood stock-still, staring at her with a heated expression. She didn't move either, too afraid of breaking the connection to even breathe. And there was a connection. She felt the tingle all the way up through her arm and down to her toes. Felt it between her legs, too. The attraction, the desire. This man had a power over her that she couldn't resist. Not wholly.

Thaus, his eyes staying on hers the entire time, slowly took the plates from her hand. Not touching her. Not moving close. Just relieving her burden. Ariel stood frozen in place, her hand on his arm. The need to feel and stroke and grab making her positively tremble.

"Baby?" Thaus said, his voice low and soothing.

"I'm not ready." The words were a whisper, a plea, and a lie all in one.

"Then don't."

Ariel swallowed hard, her heart racing and her breathing shallow. "But I want… I need."

Thaus inched a single step back so he could lean a hip against the counter, still not reaching for her. Not pushing. "So, take. I'm here for you, and I promised not to push."

She shivered, the thought of touching him, of running her hands all over all that muscular flesh making her wet. "I don't think I can."

He practically seduced her with his voice, almost pulled her in with nothing more than the sound of his own desires. "Yeah, you can. Just touch me, baby. I'm right here, and I'm not moving. I'm not going to hurt you. Take what you need from me."

So she did. She touched. She ran her fingertips up and over his arm. Slowly at first, then gaining more speed, flattening her hand to feel every inch she passed. Thaus didn't move, just as he'd promised. Though his eyes followed her hand like a man hunting. Like a predator stalking its prey. He watched, and she touched.

His skin was warm under her hand, hard and soft all at the same time. The slight hair on his forearm tickled a bit, but it was the flex of the muscles underneath his skin that made her want to sigh. He was solid, almost impossibly so. Every sinewy line of muscle led to another, overlapped and twisted with others. There was no getting around it—the man was buff.

When her fingers reached the bottom edge of his T-shirt,

she glanced up and licked her lips. Unsure. Unable to say the words she wanted to. Asking permission in the only way she could.

"Anything, baby," Thaus murmured, his hands clenching the edge of the counter. Knuckles white with the stress and arms locked at his sides. She believed him. In that moment, with him standing as strong and sure as he was, she knew he wouldn't push her. Wouldn't go too far. She could touch everything, and he'd stand there and take it. The power that knowledge gave her was definitely something new, and she liked it.

Ariel slipped her hand under the shirt and spread her fingers across his abs. The muscles there made her mouth water, made her body clench on nothing. Good gracious, so many muscles. So much strength all in one man. Her second hand joined the first as Thaus began to tremble. She was unable to resist the call of his flesh. Needed more with every exposed bit.

"Thaus," she whispered, inching closer. He growled soft and dark, a low, thrumming sound that she swore she could feel right between her legs. "I don't know…"

"Anything," he said again. Still holding himself back. Still clutching the edge of the counter like some sort of lifeline. Ariel swallowed hard and allowed herself to move closer, keeping a few inches of space between them.

"Can you…" She paused again, her skin warm and itching for something just out of reach. Her heart racing. Finally, she closed her eyes and let go. "Can you touch me, too?"

The silence was deafening, the tension between them so strong, she was held in place by the weight of it. Would he? Would he give her this? Would he risk what they'd built to satisfy what was basically her curiosity? Because she might not welcome his touch in the end, she might panic at the thought and run. She didn't want to, but her mind was a wasteland of land mines she had no way to know how to get around. Touching Thaus was tiptoeing through at a slow pace. Letting him touch her was driving a tank across the land. In the dark. With no navigation.

When she opened her eyes again, Thaus was staring down at her. Unmoving. The look in his eyes, though. The heat. He wanted this. Wanted to touch. She just needed to convince him she could handle it…convince herself.

"Please."

His expression broke, that heat simmering lower even as he shivered at her plea. "You don't need to beg."

Ariel waited as he raised his hand, as he slowly moved his fingers toward her. As he gave her an out. She stood and she fought her fear because the desire to feel him, truly feel him, was so much stronger.

"I'll never hurt you," he whispered, his words an oath, his voice a commitment.

"I think I know that."

"Someday, you'll be sure." He pushed her hair off her shoulder, still not touching her skin. Ariel trembled under his gaze, anticipation putting more pressure on her body. How could she tell him to move faster? How could she push him to do what she'd been telling him not to?

But Thaus was not a man who needed pushing. He kept his eyes on hers as his hand came up, as his fingers brushed across her jaw. A soft, fleeting touch that set her entire body on fire. She gasped, her pulse pounding. Her skin aching for more.

"Okay?" he asked.

Ariel nodded, leaning in. Feeling more than just okay. The next touch was bigger, more than just fingertips. He ran his palm along the column of her neck, cupping it almost. A dominating move for sure, but one she appreciated. That touch felt as if he was holding her, as if he had her. Supported her. As if he was solely responsible for everything around them. She needed more touches like that.

"I've got you," he whispered, pulling her softly toward him. She gave in to that pull, of course. Who wouldn't? The man was a beast, but he was hers. A gentle giant when he needed to be. And right then, as his fingers pressed into the back of her neck, she needed that from him. Needed his solid sureness and his quiet way of being. She needed him to be her mate, to understand her needs, and to deliver on his promises. He looked at her in ways that made her ache for this, and fear or no fear, she was giving in. If just for this one moment. So long as he let her.

So she moved closer, and she allowed herself to fall against him.

Thaus twisted slightly right before she made contact, just enough to keep his lower body from touching hers. A kind move on his part, or something else? Was he hard for her? Did he desire her as much as she desired him? Would she ever get to the point that she'd want to find out? She hoped she would. She really did, especially once her skin met his.

Because feeling Thaus against her was pure and utter bliss.

Ariel surrendered to her need to touch him in the most complete way she could think of, but Thaus didn't take advantage. He didn't grind on her or slide his hands under her clothing. No. Her big, strong mate let her fall against his chest so she could hug him. Full body, arms all the way around, holding tight as his head came down so he could nuzzle into her neck, Ariel held on to that big body with everything she had as he stood still and curved into hers. A bear hug, though one-sided.

And she loved it.

Every bit of tension, of fear, faded away as she held Thaus. There was no more threat coming, no more past haunting her. There was just him and her wrapped together as best they could in the kitchen of a cabin in the woods. Alone and quiet and…peaceful.

His breathing slowed, growing deeper as he relaxed into the embrace. His warmth seeped into her very soul, and the comfort that came from feeling his skin on hers, to satisfying the first step of the mating bond, brought a sense of content-ment she'd never experienced.

"You okay, baby?" he asked after several minutes of silent embracing. Ariel smiled and nodded against his chest. Not risking words at a time like this. Not needing them.

"Good," he replied. "I want to get closer, though. Can I move us?"

Ariel nodded again, not at all apprehensive, too high on the feel of him in her arms to allow her fears to take over. Without waiting for words, Thaus lifted her and took two steps to set her ass on the island counter. Never letting go. Never allowing even an inch of space between them. Her legs wrapped almost of their own accord around his hips, pulling him in deep even as he rested his hands against the counter to keep from hugging her back. Pressing all sorts of parts of him against the hottest parts of hers. And that touch, that fiery meeting of hard and soft, was everything.

"Thaus," she whispered as she rocked her hips into his very hard, very present erection. He grunted but didn't move, didn't respond. Didn't acknowledge if that felt good. Shit. "Sorry."

He growled and slid his hands down to her ass, pull-ing her in tighter before releasing her once more. Almost rubbing his cock against her. "Never apologize for trying to make yourself feel good."

But quiet bliss had been replaced by something else. Something hotter and needier, something wanting. Some-thing that gave her more courage than she'd thought pos-sible. "I was hoping it felt good for you, too."

"Just being in the same room feels good, baby. Being here, in your arms, with you letting me be this close?" He edged ever closer, tilting his hips to make her gasp just right. "It's heaven."

Ariel leaned back so she could look at him, and then she rocked her hips again. Harder. "And this? Is this heaven, too?"

He grunted softly and shook his head all slow. "This is sin, pure and simple. Beautiful, perfect sin."

But when he moved as if to hold her, as if to wrap an arm around her, the perfect little bubble cracked. Panic sputtered to life in her mind, and she jerked away from him.

"Sorry. I can't… I'm—"

Thaus was nothing if not understanding, though. He let her move back, gave her room to breathe again. To calm. He gave her space so she could move closer once more.

"I didn't mean to scare you. Tell me if I do something wrong." Thaus nuzzled her neck, locking his arms on the counter once more as he began thrusting softly against her. Giving her what she needed without pushing her too far. Hopefully, taking for himself as well.

That consideration, that understanding of her needs, was something she'd never experienced. Thaus got her in a way other men couldn't, and that made her want him all the more. So she clung to his hard body, and she worked herself against his hard cock. And she died a little bit right there against him.

Her orgasm took almost no time at all to wash over her. The mating haze and Thaus' innate sensuality definitely helped with that. She gasped and clung to her mate as he kept rocking, as he kept grunting softly into her neck, kept giving her what she needed. What she wanted. But when she was done, sated and saggy and half exhausted from the emotional and physical climb, he was still hard.

"Shouldn't you—"

"Don't worry about me." He took a step back, just enough so he could adjust himself in his pants. Obviously not wanting to go too far just yet.

But Ariel hated knowing she hadn't done enough. He'd given her pleasure, taken his time with her, coddled her broken self, and followed her emotional rules. He deserved more than a case of blue balls. And for the first time in a very long time, she wanted to please someone else. She wanted to let go and give of her body. She wanted more. For him.

Ariel slid her hand between them, earning a growl from Thaus.

"What are you doing there, baby?"

"Touching." Her fingers hit the waistband of his jeans, pausing for just a moment before slipping underneath. "More touching."

Thaus stood frozen in place, breathing hard as he let her do what she wanted. What she needed. Still not touching her.

Ariel brushed the head of his cock with the backs of her fingers, the wetness of precome making her ache in an entirely new way. She wanted a taste of him. He jerked at her touch, a tiny whine escaping his throat when she wrapped her fingers around the head. Something that made her grin.

"You okay there?" she asked as she ran a fingertip along the ridge.

"Fuck," he hissed with a thrust of his hips. "You damn well know it."

Yeah, she did. Ariel slid her hand farther inside, gripping him at the base and tugging upward. Loving the way he shivered against her. Her position was awkward, and she was beginning to think about climbing off the counter so she could get on her knees, when his hand landed on her thigh.

And her world came to a screeching halt.

Her thoughts shattered, her control disappearing in a

split second. One touch, one tiny move by him, and she was right back there. In that hell. Alone.

"Don't," she spat, burying herself in guilt when his entire body pulled away. When he practically jumped across the floor to lean once more against the opposite bank of cabinets. "I don't want to stop, but I can't handle that. Just… don't. You can't hold me down."

Thaus' eyes stayed locked on hers, his expression unreadable. She knew how hard this would be, how difficult a physical relationship would be to develop if she couldn't stand the feel of his hand on her body, but she wanted to try. She wanted to explore her boundaries with him. To seek out comfort and healing in the mating bond bringing them together. She just wasn't ready to dive in completely yet. And she couldn't stand the thought of being held in place…in any way.

But Ariel should have known Thaus would get it. His response was a simple nod and a whispered, "Okay, baby. Whatever you need."

Ariel shook her head and hopped off the counter, pressing herself against his chest once more. Seeking that state of bliss he'd given her earlier. Hoping she hadn't ruined it. "I'm sorry. I just…I can't be held down. They would wrap chains around us…on these hard tables…and they'd hold us down so one could—"

But she couldn't finish her thought. Couldn't dig through her grief to those memories. She didn't want to.

"I'll never hold you down, baby. I swear to you. And they won't ever get anywhere near you. No one like that will." Thaus kissed the top of her head, his movements slow, and his hands gripping the countertop once more. Giving her a chance to recover. Giving her everything she needed and asking for nothing in return.

Thirteen

Thaus couldn't decide if he'd been shot straight into heaven or hell. Balancing the sexual need within his mate as well as her fears and his own rage at what those bastards had done to her was an impossible conundrum. How could he please her without frightening her? How could he ease her desires without destroying the fragile bond between them? Everything with her ended up being some sort of exquisite torture, a lust-fueled roller coaster that sometimes ended in a way he hadn't seen coming. One hand on her leg, and they'd crashed. That was all it took.

But his mate, she rallied hard, which only caused more confusion. He had Ariel pressed up against him with her legs spread around him…and he couldn't touch her. Not really. He'd slipped with the hand on her thigh, and her reaction had been immediate and visceral in its fear. A fact that just about killed him. She seemed so shattered by what they did to her. Thaus wanted to fix that, to help her find some sort of comfort, but he had no idea if he ever would. No one healed from being treated so violently. They moved on and learned to live with the memories and the nightmares, but they never truly healed. Those scars ran too deep to disappear. Instead, they stood out, scabbed and swollen. Always one touch away from breaking open again. From lashing out with renewed pain. People who'd been so broken didn't heal; they learned to live through the pain and the mess of a cycle of fear most people would never experience. They soldiered on even when they had no idea how to do so. They survived because the other option wasn't an option at all.

Thaus stood completely still, watching Ariel, waiting her out. She seemed so much smaller as she collected herself, so breakable. He knew her strength, though. He saw it on her face every moment of the day. She battled demons he could only imagine, led by a sense of determination that eclipsed everything around her. She was more powerful than he was by far, just for being willing to get out of bed every morning and face what the day would bring.

Ariel proved that strength when she once again slid her fingers into his waistband. Brave to the point of pain, his shewolf.

Thaus jerked back, clenching his hand into a fist so he wouldn't reach for her. "You don't have to—"

"I know, but I want to," she said, once again getting to know his cock with her fingers. A warrior fighting a battle in her own mind as she tried to push past something he could never truly understand.

The heaven of her touch once again warred with the hell of not being able to reciprocate in any way. He growled and dropped his head, unsure about continuing but unable to resist. Her hand felt so good, too good almost. Felt like the breath of an angel from a place he'd never thought he'd make it into. Just the sight of her, the peeks he managed of what she was doing, was almost enough to push him over the edge.

He thrust into her grip slowly, holding back as much as he could so as not to scare her again. Grunting softly when the head slid through her fist.

"You have to tell me," he said as he rocked faster. "Let me know if I push you too much."

"I will." She grabbed his T-shirt, fisting the fabric to bring him closer. Pushing her own boundaries, it seemed. For his mate was out to prove something, whether to him or herself, he didn't know. But Ariel was a woman on a mission, and he was the one benefiting from that objective.

Thaus was far more careful this time with where he put his hands. Not on her, that was for sure. Instead, he grabbed the counter by the edge and held on. Hoping he could control himself and remember not to touch her. To wait for her to ask.

But as the pleasure climbed up his spine and his sac tightened against his body, he knew that was going to be a tough one. Already, his arms itched to hold her, his hands dying to run over her skin. She had his cock in her hand and her breasts against his chest, yet he somehow managed to hold himself back.

He should be a goddamned saint after this hand job if he managed not to grab her.

"Fuck, baby." His legs shook with his oncoming orgasm. He was going to come so hard, much harder than ever before from a simple hand job. He knew it was all because of her, his mate, his one true match. Ariel's touch ignited him in ways no one else's could, and bonding sexually with her was something he wanted with a desperation he almost couldn't fathom.

The mating haze danced around them both, clouding Thaus' mind and driving him down a road of pleasure and desire he couldn't have turned off of if he'd wanted to. And he didn't. The mating imperative kept them together, kept him rocking into her touch, kept him wanting more. And his mate? She seemed just as affected. Just as wild and needy.

He had no idea if they'd be able to stop. Ever.

But before he could finish in her hand, before he could even realize what the hell she was doing, Ariel yanked him forward. He stumbled, crashing into the opposite bank of cabinets and grasping the edge of the counter hard once again. His mate, his shy, beautiful mate, had the look of a wild animal about her. Eyes bright, breaths coming fast. Feral.

"What's wrong?" he asked as he turned to face her. As he readied himself for anything.

"Want more," she said with a sexy-as-fuck growl, her hands shaking. "I'm... Thaus, I'm scared, but I want... I need."

He wasn't quite prepared for that, though. Heaven and hell, together again. He knew what she needed, knew exactly what it was she wanted, but there was no way she was ready. He refused to even consider sex an option at that point because the woman was in a sort of frenzy that would feed his own desire. It would make him careless and blanket her with far more confidence than she had. The mating haze had convinced Ariel she was ready, but Thaus knew the opposite to be true. He couldn't take her.

But he could give himself to her. He could surrender to her needs and let her do whatever she felt she needed. Give her the time and the space to work through her fears of touch and intimacy. He could, and he would. For her.

"Okay," Thaus said finally, surrendering to her need as best he could. He leaned back, gripped the edge of the countertop, and spread his legs a little wider. "I'm right here, baby. I'm right here, not moving, and I'm all yours. What do you need? What is it I can give to you to make you feel better?"

Ariel whimpered a sound that tore through his heart. But in the next moment, she dropped to her knees and dove

SAVAGE SILENCE • 111

for his pants. He held completely still, watching her, unable to look away from the sight of his mate on her knees before him. Owning him from a submissive position. She had the power. She held all the cards and told him what game to play. And when her tongue came out to taste the head of him, he almost died for the sixth time in his very long life.

"Holy fuck," he murmured, hanging on tight to the stone counter. "Baby, you're killing me."

She placed her hands on his thighs, gripping him tightly as she balanced against him. Teasing him with her touch and warmth. She leaned in slowly, teasingly so. Keeping her eyes on his as she opened her mouth. As she stopped the entire world with the look she shot him. And when she finally reached him, when she moved close enough, she wrapped her lips around the head of his cock, and she sucked. Hard.

Thaus moaned and jerked at the pleasure shooting straight up his spine, dying inside at the heat and the wet and the delicious fucking pressure. His mate, his stunning, shy, strong as fuck mate, had his cock in her mouth and was pulling him in deep. And she never once looked away while doing it. The sight, the sensation, the way she willingly swallowed him down—it was too much. He wanted to fuck her. No teasing, no foreplay, no soft words. He wanted to throw her ass on the counter and thrust inside. Wanted to slide deep and fuck her until she screamed. Until he made her come on his cock.

But none of that could happen just yet, and there, once again, was the hell with his slice of heaven.

"That's it," he hissed as she licked the slit before taking him back inside. "Fuck, you feel so good. Do you like that?"

She moaned around him, sucking him in once more. Just the tip this time. Just enough to make him want to claw at her head and push himself deeper. He grabbed the counter harder and held on for dear life instead. He was going to come. He was going to come so hard. His claws erupted from his fingers, burying themselves in the underside of the stone counter as his hips jerked forward. In the next moment, a huge snap sounded through the kitchen, making them both jump. Making Ariel pull away and leave his poor, soaking wet cock standing all alone and needy.

"Oops," Thaus said with a shrug. He'd broken the slab of stone on the counter behind him, snapped it right in two. Not that he gave a shit. Collateral damage wasn't something he was concerned about at that moment. Ariel stared, still on her knees, her face so fucking close to his cock he almost begged for her to return to what she was doing.

But apparently, the gods of timing and opportunity would have rather seen him in hell. The sound of an incoming, low-flying helicopter sounded deep and dark through the otherwise quiet morning. The thumping of the blades moving closer at a high rate of speed.

"Shit," Thaus said, tucking himself away and fastening his pants. "We've got company."

Ariel jumped to her feet, looking terrified and almost panicked. Thaus wanted to reach for her, to calm her, but he knew that was the wrong move. Instead, he herded her back against the island and leaned over her. Not touching, but surrounding.

"It's more than likely my pack, but let me go make sure, okay?"

She nodded, still looking all kiss-swollen and sex-hazed. And scared. Fuck, he hated to walk away from her even for a second, especially when she might need calming as the sex haze lifted. When she might need him to reassure her that nothing had changed, that he'd still wait for her, that he wouldn't push her. Bad fucking timing was an understatement for the arrival of his team.

He nuzzled her neck and gave her a reassuring growl before pulling away. "I'll be right back."

"You're not supposed to say that."

"What?"

"That horror movie thing. You're never supposed to say I'll be right back."

He stared down at her, wanting to smile at that little show of strength, at the display of something almost normal. Instead, he leaned in a little closer to whisper in her ear. "I can say it because it's true. I haven't slid my tongue into your pussy yet, and there's no way I'm dying before I get that chance."

He cocked a grin her way then hurried out the back door. He was going to have a raging case of blue balls in about ten minutes, but there was nothing he could do about that. His team was here.

As the chopper rose from where it must have dropped the Dires off, gaining altitude for the journey south, Phego came over the far hill. Tall and as thick as the rest of them, his brother looked the most like a serial killer in his opinion. Cold eyes, an almost expressionless face, and an air of something downright diabolical tended to keep people away from him. He was the man to go to when you needed something no one else thought you could get. Relentless was a good word for Phego, and Thaus was awfully glad to have him in his corner.

"See anything?" Thaus hollered when he knew the other Dire could hear him.

"A wall of fucking mud ready to come down. Otherwise, nada."

"The mud could work in our favor."

Mammon followed Phego through the trees, appearing like a shadow of the other Dire. "You could blow the fucker, T. Block the bastards from making it up the mountain."

"Yeah, that's my thought."

"You'd bury the attackers," Mammon said.

"But it'd block us in, too," Phego added. "Rough mountains to the south, ocean to the west, and an almost impossible range to the east? That's not exactly a great place to be. We could end up trapped pretty easily."

"Trapped with a newly mated couple?" Mammon shivered. "Fuck and no. Did that once, remember?"

All three men grimaced and said, "Levi," at the same time. That was one shared memory none of them wanted to revisit. Hell, Thaus had been injured during that time, had been laid up with the shot to his shoulder, and still, he remembered the sounds of nonstop sex coming from the bedroom of the little cabin.

Not again, even if he was the one getting lucky.

"What's the situation with your mate?" Phego asked, breaking Thaus from his own thoughts.

Thaus sighed. There was a certain difficulty to telling them anything about Ariel. Her secrets were his to protect, but the guys needed to understand her. Needed to know why they'd have to take down the Glaxious pack for her without ever touching her. They needed the basics.

"The fucking Omega stealers had her."

"Shit," Mammon growled. "Was she at Merriweather when the battle went down?"

"No. She escaped before that. But they…" He shook his head, unable to say the words. But his team had been together a long time, and they had an understanding most men didn't. So Thaus took a deep breath and looked each one in the eye, making sure his words carried the hate and the disgust they deserved for what they meant to his mate. "She doesn't like to be touched anymore."

Phego snarled, his entire body stiff with what could only be rage. Mammon wasn't much better. He stared, shocked, obviously taking an extra moment to fully grasp the meaning behind the words. Because Thaus wouldn't be graphic, he couldn't. If Thaus said the word, if he told them those bastards had raped his mate, he might give in to a fury that would never let him go. And that was the last thing Ariel needed.

"Motherfuckers," Mammon growled, cracking his neck and looking ready to battle at any second. Phego, well, he calmed quickly. He was more observant than the rest of his brothers, more tactical. While Mammon would rage just like Thaus, Phego would settle and look over every option. Would think through exactly how to deal with a threat. And then he'd destroy it.

"You solid?" Phego asked, looking Thaus over with concerned eyes. Thaus knew what his brother meant. Phego probably sensed how close to the edge he was, probably knew what any one of them would want to do in a similar situation. He was making sure Thaus had control before they dealt with what was coming.

"Trying to be," Thaus said, which was the only answer he could give.

"Are the men who did the damage taken care of?"

Thaus hated to answer that one. "Not sure. But the immediate threat is the Glaxious wolves."

Mammon snarled deep, looking out into the wilderness as if seeking the threat they all knew was coming. "Fucking bastards aren't coming anywhere near her."

"Not on our watch," Phego added, nodding his promise to Thaus. "Ooh Rah."

Fourteen

*G*riel felt as if she'd somehow awakened a beast and tamed him all at the same time.

She stared at the broken counter, completely transfixed by the cracks and curves of where the two pieces had once met. Thaus had done that, had gotten worked up enough to break a piece of stone in half. Simply because of what she'd been doing to him. The thrill that gave her, the power that coursed through her at the very idea of controlling such a man…she liked it. A lot.

She feared it, too.

Her needs were building, and the mating imperative set forth by the bond between them was growing to the point that it almost eclipsed her reservations. Not completely yet, but close. Soon. It helped that Thaus was so understanding and patient. He'd broken a stone countertop while holding himself in place. Kept his hands away when she asked him to. He hadn't pushed her to touch or be touched; he'd simply let her play as she wanted to and minded her rules when she laid them out. Being a hulking, quiet, burly man, he had a sensitive side she hadn't seen coming. And that might end up being what would finally push her over the edge.

"Ariel."

She spun at his voice, her heart flying and her breath catching. He leaned in through the door, watching her, not moving. He looked as if he knew he'd scared her, and she felt horrible about that. She'd been so wrapped up in the countertop and possibilities…

"Yeah?" Her voice came out soft, but it didn't wobble. She took a deep breath and inched closer to him, wanting to feel him again. Her hands itching to touch. This need to complete the mating wasn't easy to keep under control.

"Are you okay?"

"Yeah. Totally. Just jumpy."

"Because my packmates are strangers?"

She hadn't really had time to think about that yet, but once he brought it up, the nervous flutters began in her chest. "Probably."

Thaus grunted, shooting a quick glance over his shoulder. "I was going to invite them inside to meet you, but it can wait."

Way to be a jackass, girl. "No. Let them come in. I'll be fine."

But as he turned to leave, one more thought struck her. One that induced a sense of panic that had her leaping across the kitchen in a very inhuman way. She landed right by the door and reached for him. Voluntarily running her fingers along his arm. Needing his touch to soothe her frazzled nerves.

"You'll be with me, right? When they…when they're here."

Thaus stared at her fingers on his forearm, his eyes intense but his face giving nothing away. "Every fucking second."

"Good. Okay." The weight on her chest lifted, letting

her breathe again. Her emotions seemed to fall over the map. She'd need to address that if she was going to pull off appearing as a regular, sane woman. Bolstering herself to once again bear the brunt of separation, she took a single step back, breaking their tentative physical connection. "Then, yeah, I can meet them."

But when he walked outside, the sense of safety and security he'd given her went with him. Ariel could barely breathe without gasping, could hardly hold still from the tremors in her hands. She was a walking, talking panic attack, and that wouldn't do. Refusing to give in to her fears, she hurried behind the island. She felt a need for a barrier between her and these new men, wanted something to be in the way should they…do something.

She didn't even know what it was that made her so afraid of them.

Thaus walked through the door a moment later, followed by two men who looked a lot like him on first pass. Tall, thick, muscular…poster children for soldiers and bodyguards. One had lighter hair, though, and wore it in a longer cut. The other was darker in look and the air about him. Rougher, though not as rough as her Thaus. Still, he'd be the one to worry about.

"Ariel, this is Mammon." Thaus pointed to the lighter man. "And Phego." Another point, this time to the darker, scary one.

Thaus came to her side, keeping a few inches between them but standing close enough to provide that blanket of security she desperately needed. "Brothers, this is Ariel. She's a doctor for humans and shifters, and she's an endurance-running wolf with enough energy to keep up with me through these hills." He glanced down at her, his eyes swirling with color like she'd never seen before. Going almost silver. "She's also my mate."

Ariel heard the wolf in his voice, sensed the beast close to the surface of his mind. That sound, that instinct, comforted her.

She inched closer and nodded. "Hi."

"I don't know how you got stuck with this big lug," Mammon said, smiling. "But good luck to you, sweetheart."

Phego watched her with a single-minded interest that flared every instinct she had, making her bones want to crawl out of her skin. She moved closer to Thaus, brushing his side before she even realized what she was doing. He didn't jump or wrap an arm around her as most men probably would have. No, he stood solid and still, supporting her, waiting on her. Calming her with his touch and his presence at her side. In a moment of peace and desire that overshadowed her fears, she reached for him. Grabbed his hand and held on. Hers felt so small inside his massive one, but they fit somehow. And when he squeezed her, when his fingers cupped over hers, when he held on to her in a way that wasn't terrifying, she felt at home. Finally.

"We should patrol," Phego said, breaking his silence and the warm, happy feelings she'd been sinking into. Ariel's immediate sense of discomfort around the man flared hotter and brighter. Burning her up inside. He would not be her favorite.

"I want to check the potential mudslide area you mentioned," Thaus said, still holding her hand but going all hard and mission-focused in an instant. "See if there's a logical way to blow it and get an idea of the damage and reward if we did."

"I'm in on that. I love to see the master work," Mammon said with a grin. But then his smile fell, and all three men turned to look right at her.

That uncomfortable sensation came back with a vengeance. "What?"

Thaus sighed and squeezed her hand. "I don't want to leave you alone."

"So, don't. I can go wi—"

"No," he spat before she could even finish her sentence. "That's too dangerous. As is leaving you alone."

And in that moment, as he stared down at her with his eyes filled with concern, the dilemma became clear. He wanted to patrol, needed to. Not like earlier, when he'd been able to stay close enough to the cabin to monitor her. No, he needed to roam farther. To spend some time in an area where he couldn't immediately get back to her if she needed him. A thought that didn't sit well with her, either. But this was his job, and he needed to go. Which meant she needed to be able to stay alone with a stranger. A man.

She needed to be able to lie well enough to convince him she'd be okay.

Ariel squared her shoulders and lifted her chin, calling on every bit of strength and stubbornness that had gotten her through medical school at a time when women simply didn't do such things. The same mind-set that gave her the courage to survive every day in that torture camp until she escaped.

She called on that, and she forced a smile on her face because her mate needed her to be okay. "I'll be fine no matter what you decide."

Thaus stared down at her for a long minute, watching and weighing. Probably expecting a sign of weakness to appear. But Ariel was far too stubborn to let that happen. He needed her to be strong, and damn it, she wouldn't let him down.

When she didn't break under his scrutiny, he nodded. "Okay, then."

Success.

Thaus glanced at the other males. "Mammon and I will

patrol this round, then we'll switch to make sure all three of us know the terrain and the plan. The last thing we need is one of us getting caught up in the slide."

"On it," Mammon said as he headed for the door. "It was nice to meet you, Ariel. See you later."

"Sure." Ariel tried to sound casual and confident, but she felt anything but. So she faked it, and she clung to Thaus' hand in a way that kept them touching but not too much. She couldn't break her act.

"You okay?" Thaus asked when she didn't let him go, his voice low and quiet. Almost a whisper.

"Fine." She gritted her teeth and plastered a smile on her face. Still clinging.

"I don't have to go."

"Nope. I'm good. I can do this." And she could. She had to. She finally let go of her mate, stepping out from behind the counter on knees about as supportive as jelly so she could address Phego directly. "Can I get you something to drink or eat?"

Phego glanced at Thaus, then back to her. "Uh, sure. Ice water would be great."

She nodded and moved about the kitchen, grabbing ice and filling a glass with water. She was about to hand it to him, about to pass it off, when he took a step forward. The size of him, the hulking shadow he cast as he stepped under the overhead light, made her gasp and jerk back. The glass fell from her hands and shattered on the hard floor.

And just like that, she knew she'd failed.

"That's it," Thaus said as he grabbed a towel.

"I'm sorry," Ariel whispered, rushing to her knees so she could pick up the glass. "I'm not usually so jumpy. It's just—"

"Stop." Phego knelt beside her, his hand outstretched as if reaching for her but not closing the gap. Holding himself in check. "You'll cut yourself. And don't apologize. It's my fault for not being more cautious when I sensed you were a bit skittish. I'm the one who should be sorry."

"Phego, go with Mammon and get a good understanding of the terrain. We can figure something out for me to be able to investigate the slide later." Thaus joined her, moving her hands aside and grabbing the largest pieces of glass himself. "I've got this."

"On it." Phego left without another word, joining Mammon outside. Leaving the mated pair on the floor of the kitchen.

Ariel sagged, the weight of her failure heavy and hard to carry. "I am so sorry."

"Don't," he replied, his word a growl in the air as he got to his feet. A warning...one she didn't take.

"No, really." Ariel stood and followed him toward the trash can. "I feel like such an ass. Your brothers are going to think I'm a nutcase."

Thaus spun, snarling loud, stalking closer. A man pissed off and ready to attack. Ariel backed into the island, too turned on by his show to be afraid.

"My brothers will think you're amazing and strong for being able to survive what you did, not to mention they'll be impressed that you escaped. We saw that hell, remember? We went into the holding cabins. We pulled out the women left. We *know*." He pushed closer, his warmth bathing her even though he kept enough space between them so as not to pin her in place.

"Thaus," she whispered, having no idea what she was asking for.

His growl dropped and slowed, becoming almost purr-like. "They'll also never think poorly of you because they know I'd rip their fucking faces off if I found out."

"You say the sweetest things." Ariel leaned forward, resting her forehead against his chest. "Why am I so messed up?"

He hummed but didn't hold her tighter. Didn't move to embrace her in any way, and somehow, Ariel found herself wishing for it. Almost craving it. She inched closer, bringing her hands to his biceps. Holding him. Surrendering to the need to touch. Thaus stood absolutely still. Quiet and calm as he allowed her to take from him. Waiting. Giving her the power to do as she wanted. As she needed.

And by the gods, did she suddenly need to feel him.

Closer still, she let her breasts press into his chest. "Thaus."

He growled again, shaking a bit this time. Obviously holding back for her. And while she could understand him denying himself, why was she? She wanted to touch more of him, wanted to know how he felt against her. Why was she waiting?

When she couldn't come up with any answers, she closed her eyes and knew her waiting was over. On a single breath and in one quick move, she fell forward and wrapped herself around him.

"Please," she whispered, holding tighter. "I need to feel you. I need you to…hug me back."

It took Thaus far longer than she'd expected to move. Long enough that she'd begun to doubt he would. But then he began to curl his body over hers, slowly wrapping his arms around her back. Letting her feel his intentions and direction with every agonizing inch he claimed. And when he was finished, when he held her as tightly as she held him, her body sagged in relief. A hug. Her first hug in years.

"I can feel your tension," Thaus said, keeping his voice soft.

She snuggled closer, enjoying the warmth and the closeness. Letting her hands slide where they chose to. Letting her mind go to the place that frightened her more than just about anything at that moment. "They're coming, aren't they?"

Thaus didn't hesitate with his answer. "Yes."

"Can we stop them?"

"If we work together."

"So you'll fight them? Just the three of you against that pack?"

He pulled back, meeting her gaze with the strength of his own. "For you. I'll fight to the death for you, and my brothers will do the same because you're one of us. You're part of the Dire pack, and we never leave one of our own behind."

And somehow, she believed him.

Fifteen

Thaus wasn't sure what about that moment in the kitch-
en changed the dynamic between him and his mate. One
second, he was doing his best to keep her calm and fight the
need to touch her, and the next, he was holding her tightly.
Surrounding her smaller body with his own. Holding her up,
it seemed, as something shifted between them.

Something good, he sensed.

And hours later, after much holding, swaying, talking,
and waiting, after his brothers had come back and quickly
laid out what they'd seen before they disappeared into the
night to leave the two mated shifters alone, that shift remained. Ariel was more open to him, less walled off. And he
had no idea what that meant.

"You should get some sleep," she whispered against his
chest. The words sent a shiver up his spine. One he did his
best to control so she didn't notice.

"I will if you will."

"How can I sleep when I know they're coming for me?"

"Ditto." He gripped her hip, pulling her tighter into his embrace. "But you need to rest."

"I will if you will."

His snorted laugh brought forth a giggle from his mate. A sound he instantly fell in love with and wanted to hear more often.

"Using my words against me, huh?" He pulled back, resting his cheek against her forehead and inhaling her sweet scent. "How about I put you to bed and promise to get a little shut-eye myself once I'm sure the guys are good outside?"

"How about you check on the guys and *then* put me to bed...so you can join me there?"

It took Thaus far longer than it should have to filter through the letters and syllables, to find meaning among the phonetics. And when he did, when her words finally made sense to him, he locked his body in place.

"There's only one bed."

Ariel ran her nails across the width of his shoulders in a move that made his cock swell in an almost painful way. "I know. I slept in it already, remember?"

Think, idiot. Think...with your brain. "We'd have to share it."

"I figured that out as well." Her hands slid across his hips and up his back, pulling him slightly closer with each pass. "I'm enjoying the first hug I've felt in years. I'm not ready to end it just yet."

The heaven of her embrace, the hell of her request. Once again, his mate threw him into a pit of indecision. One that lasted far too long.

Ariel sighed. "You don't have to."

At the sadness in her voice, the shyness, he growled. "Fuck, baby. I want nothing more than to wrap you in my arms and hold you all night long. But this is still so new."

"I know," she whispered, sounding surer than he would

have expected. "But I feel it. The connection between us. I want to feed it."

Thaus sighed, eyes closing as he kissed her forehead again. This decision, this contemplation, was as brutal as any he'd ever had to make. Of *course,* he wanted to share a bed with her. To wrap her in his arms and keep her safe as she rested. That was an innate wolf instinct—to care for their mates. But as much as she may have thought she was ready, Thaus worried she wasn't. What if he crawled into bed and she panicked? Or worse, she completely retreated behind the walls she'd built around herself? He refused to push her, to make her fear him, to do something that would unravel the fragile bond between them.

But how could he refuse her without making it seem as if he was overriding her decision?

"I'll make you a deal," he said as he pulled himself out of her embrace. "You get ready for bed, and I'll check in with my pack. When I come back, if you still want me with you, I'll...agree to share the bed."

But his words didn't seem to entice her at all. Instead, they quite obviously angered her. She crossed her arms over her chest and cocked her head in a way that screamed trouble.

"Gee, way to be enthusiastic."

"Hang on." Thaus ran his fingers over the back of her hand before encircling it in his own, larger one. Always aware of how easily his woman spooked. "Baby, there is nothing—and I mean *nothing*—I want more than you in my arms. But I'm not going to push you or do anything that might ruin what we're building here. You say you want me in your bed? I'm in...once I give you time to retract that request." He tugged her closer, looping one arm around her hips in a slow and precise move he prayed wouldn't be a trigger. "You are my priority, always. I don't want you to feel pressured in any way."

Ariel sighed, sagging into his hold. "Okay. I get it."

"Do you?"

"Totally." She pulled back and smiled up at him. "Go check in. I'll be waiting in the bedroom for you."

"Hmmm." He leaned in for a quick kiss—their first one—before practically breaking his soul in two to back away from her. "Give me ten minutes."

His mate sent him a smile he saw right through. "Okay."

"I promise," he said as he opened the door. "Ten minutes, tops."

"I'll be counting."

Me too, he thought as he stepped out into the night. Thaus took a deep breath and held it before sighing. What a couple of days. What a glorious, confusing, perfectly madhouse time. One he doubted he would ever forget, for it was when his Ariel came blasting through his life.

It took him longer to force himself off the back porch than it did to find Phego. The Dire was closer than Mammon, sitting in the darkness of the woods a mere hundred yards from the cabin.

"You pull easy duty tonight?" Thaus asked as he walked up to the spot where he knew the wolf would be. He couldn't see the beast yet, but he sensed him. Smelled him, too.

"Mammon still owed me from that bullshit in Texas he pulled when he met Charmeine. I'm finally collecting," Phego said once he shifted to his human form. "What's up?"

Thaus stared out across the wild lands below them, even his wolf vision not giving him much of a view. "I wanted to check in."

"We've got this. Go take care of your mate."

But Thaus' mind had begun to spin, thoughts of the next day and the strategies they'd decided upon creating static and noise. The truth too loud to ignore. "I'm the weapons expert, the only one trained in high-level explosives. I'm going to have to set the charges."

Phego must have understood exactly where Thaus' mind had gone because he didn't miss a single beat in responding. "Yep, which is why you should take advantage of your time with Ariel now. Come tomorrow, we can't have you backing out because she gets scared. As much as we all want her safe and calm and trusting of us, we've got shit to do that requires your attention. She can't impede that."

Thaus growled, the harsh sound breaking the still night apart. "Don't judge her for her fears. She's obviously got some sort of PTSD."

"Yeah, I know. I figured that out within fifteen seconds of meeting her." Phego stood and leaned against a tree, arms crossed over his chest. "Tomorrow's going to be hard on all of us if she gets triggered. Whether it's me or Mammon who ends up staying with her as protection, we're going to have to deal with that pain and fear the entire time you're gone. And while I know that's nothing compared to what you'll be dealing with, feeling that through your mating bond, it's still going to be brutal. So don't think I'm faulting her for cracking under the pressure. I'm damn surprised she made it out of that hell with any sort of sanity whatsoever. And impressed."

Thaus released a breath, almost growling into the night. "Sorry. I'm…out of my element."

"No shit. Who wouldn't be?" Phego gave him a moment of silence, a few seconds' break from thinking of all the things, to just be. One that didn't last nearly long enough. "Mammon and I will take care of her when we have to, but you're the only one who can build her up enough to hang strong while we do that. Go keep her as calm and relaxed as you can tonight. We'll have your back and hers tomorrow."

Thaus had always known his brothers would come through for him no matter what, but hearing those words from Phego resonated in a way he hadn't expected. They'd take care of Ariel, of course, they would. But he had a job to do first.

"Thanks, man," Thaus said as he turned to leave Phego behind.

"Paybacks are a bitch, you know."

Thaus thought of Mammon, running through the dark, unfamiliar forest and rocky outcroppings. And he grinned. "So I've heard."

With Phego's chuckle still in his ears, Thaus hurried back to the cabin still in human form. It would have taken less time in wolf form, but his shoulder practically creaked with every swing of his arm, and he didn't want to injure it more considering the fight headed their way. If the mud and rock fell as he hoped it would, there'd be no hand-to-hand combat needed. But he wasn't relying on that one defensive maneuver to succeed completely, not when it was Ariel at risk.

Speaking of which…

His mate was standing in the kitchen when he walked inside. And she looked worried.

Thaus nearly leapt across the kitchen to her side. "Is everything okay?"

"Yeah, I just…" She shook her head, smiling up at him. "I was getting anxious."

A quick glance at the clock confirmed his suspicions—nine minutes had passed. His Ariel had probably been staring at that same clock, hopeful and filled with dread all at once.

Thaus surrendered to his need to touch her by reaching out to run his fingers over the length of her arm. "I promised."

"I know, I just…worried."

"That I wouldn't come back?"

Ariel shrugged. "I don't know."

But she did. Thaus knew she did deep inside. She worried he'd disappear from her life and she'd be left alone again, the same way he worried for her. Two sides of the same coin.

And he would do his best to make sure she understood that.

"Ariel, you are my fated mate. My perfect match. You are the one being in all of history that is the right fit to claim my heart. I will always come back for you. Whether from a fight or from death itself; nothing will ever take me from you unless you want me gone. And I pray to every god in the universe that day never comes."

— —

Ariel could hardly breathe. Something inside of her broke with Thaus' words. Something that felt like the foundation of one of the barriers she'd built within herself. The broken bits cracked and slid, causing the wall sitting atop them to fall into nothing more than a pile of rock and dust. Debris of her past littering her soul. That wall falling opened up a section of her mind she'd long since hidden away, freed thoughts and needs she'd never expected to have again. It gave her the freedom to accept that she didn't want anything between her and the man the fates had chosen for her. No mental walls or physical space, not even clothes. The mating imperative burned through her in an inferno she couldn't contain. He was preparing to fight an entire pack for her, an unknown number of shifters coming specifically for her, and she might lose him in the battle.

She was ready to accept him as hers. Fully.

"Thaus?"

"Yeah?"

But when the time came, the words refused to come.

Wall or no wall, the decision to join with him in a full mating was one that required a lot of thought and care. She wouldn't jump into it.

"I want to examine your shoulder."

Thaus appeared almost as surprised as she felt. "You... what?"

But the more she thought about it, the more sense it made. She needed to find *her* place. Her comfort zone. And she was most comfortable when she was in her role as a doctor, far more so than her new role as a mate.

"You're favoring your other arm and barely moving the one with the residual pain issues. Obviously, it's bothering you. I want to examine it." Ariel rubbed her hand over his arm, trying to find words to make this clear to him. To get him to understand. "I know who I am when I'm a doctor. Let me be her for a bit."

He sighed, seeming to sag under her very gaze. "Okay."

"Yeah?"

"Sure. Why not?" Without pausing, he yanked his shirt over his head, hopped up onto the island countertop, and lay on his chest so she could see his back. "This good?"

Her wolf practically purred. The smooth skin, the muscles, the single, ugly scar on the one side that proved his prowess and strength. Yeah, this was good. Too good.

"It's fine," she said, a little breathlessly. She started her examination by running her fingers along the puckered scar. "You said you've had multiple surgeries?"

Thaus moaned an affirmative response. "Seven. Probably needing an eighth soon if the pain is any indication."

She prodded the edges of the wound, then pressed deeper in the center. Letting the feel of muscle and bone center her on the task. "What do they do in these surgeries?"

"Rebreak the bone and try to align the joint for a smoother fit."

"But it doesn't work."

"Nope." Thaus growled in a sexy sort of way as she smoothed the palms of her hands over his shoulder. "That feels good."

And it did. The warmth of his skin under hers, the ease with which she could touch and feel him. It felt really, really good. Almost too good.

"You should let me try," she said, expanding the path of her hands. Moving from examination into exploration.

Thaus tilted his head, an odd sort of look on his handsome face. "You want to operate on me?"

"Why not?"

He shrugged, closing his eyes as she kept stroking his bare skin. "I could never do that."

"Operate?"

"Yeah. I mean, no, not *just* operate. On you, specifically. I wouldn't want to hurt you."

Ariel's heart practically sang for him. Something about his words, about the tone he used and the promise behind them, pushed her past the final hurdle holding her back. They set her free in a way that nothing else—not a single promise or a plea for her to understand—ever could have.

"Sit up," she whispered, needing to see his face.

Thaus did as she asked, and then he slid off the counter. Standing before her in all his shirtless glory. Staring down at her as if he knew what she was about to do. About to say.

"Thaus?"

"Yeah?"

Deep breath. "I want to go to bed with you."

He didn't jerk back, didn't seem shocked at all, really. He simply stood as strong and still as he always had. And he watched her as he gave her an out. "You know that means—"

"I know," she said, nodding. Holding his gaze with her own to show her truth. "I'm ready to be alone in a bed with you. To...try."

"Are you sure? I won't be the bigger person and tell you no, baby. I can't—I want you too much for that. But I'll stop no matter what. You just have to say the word."

"Of course you will," she whispered, trying hard to stay in a place of Zen-like calm. "I'm not promising perfection or even completion—the stars only know what will happen once we begin—but I want to try. I want to move forward… with you."

Thaus didn't respond with words. Instead, he grabbed her hand in his and walked backward. Pulling her down the hall to the bedroom, keeping his eyes on hers the entire time. Keeping his hand soft as he held hers. Ariel followed, knowing this was more than just any old walk. Feeling the weight of the moment in very breath and step.

Ariel closed the door behind them once they crossed the threshold to the bedroom, almost shaking in anticipation. Maybe a little fear mixed in as well. It'd been so long, and she'd been so certain she would never be able to do this again. Never be able to experience the touch of a man on her flesh, the pleasure that came from affection and the joy of true intimacy. She'd assumed she'd die never revisiting sex with a partner.

No longer.

"I don't know if I'm ready," she said, breaking the heavy silence between them.

"I know, but I'm not them," Thaus said as his hands went to his waistband. "I'll never be them."

"I know that." Ariel pulled her shirt off, wanting to make sure he took her seriously. That he didn't doubt her. Needing to be the one to go first. Thaus followed, the two of them slowly stripping in front of each other. Not speaking. Not helping. Just…baring it all. Leaving the layers of their clothes piled on the floor along with the reservations holding each other back.

And when they were naked—when each had taken away the barriers between them—Thaus waited again for her to make the decision. To be comfortable in the direction they took. This was her show, and he was making sure she knew that at every stage.

"I want this," she whispered as she headed to the bed. "I want you as my mate."

"So have me."

"And if I'm not ready?" She wasn't, not quite. Not yet. And she bet he already knew it.

"Then we lie together. Or we sleep. Or we get dressed and play Parcheesi."

"Parcheesi?"

He shrugged in a casual, confident sort of way that only he could have pulled off. "It's all I could think up on such short notice."

"Do you know how to play Parcheesi?"

"No."

Ariel glanced down, staring at his chest to gain the confidence to look back into his eyes as she asked the hardest question of all. "Do you know how to get me to calm down so I can do more than stand here completely terrified?"

Thaus glanced at the bed and held out a hand. "Yeah, I think I do."

Sixteen

Thaus couldn't look away from Ariel. There was something so sweet about her request, so telling. She wanted this, but her mind hadn't completely cut off yet. The battle to balance her need to protect herself versus the mating imperative appeared to be a rough one, but she fought hard. And he could be the potential winner in the whole thing.

"Lie with me," he said, keeping his voice calm and low. Soothing almost.

"We're naked."

"That's okay. We can be naked without doing anything more than getting to know one another. Just lie with me."

It took her longer to agree than he wanted, but eventually, she took that first step. Crossed the few inches needed to meet him. He led her to the bed, giving her space to crawl in and find a comfortable spot. The image of her naked and in those white sheets rocked him, but he didn't react. Not intentionally. His cock jutted upward, hard and straining, but there was nothing he could do about that. Nothing he wanted to do other than bury himself inside her, which still wasn't an option. Not yet.

When Ariel finally lay still, looking up at him with those eyes he wanted to fall into, he joined her on that big, white slice of heaven. He lay with his head on a pillow and her in front of him. Keeping space between them to give her time to adjust.

"You can come closer," Ariel whispered. Once again bridging the gap between them, though this time, with her words. Thaus didn't answer, didn't feel the need to. He simply inched forward until their bodies only just touched. Until her warmth enveloped him more completely than the blankets could have.

"Better?" Thaus asked. Her arm around his waist was one of the best feelings in the entire world, and her hip rubbing against the head of his cock was one of the most painful. But in an amazing sort of way.

"Yeah. Better." Ariel chuckled softly, looking almost innocent as she grinned at him. "You know you're huge, right?"

Yeah, he did. But still… "No. What are you talking about?"

Ariel's cheeks darkened, and she reached a hand out to run a single finger over the length of him.

"This," she whispered, the sound making his balls pull up tight. "I mean, you're big all over, but this…"

Thaus had to close his eyes, had to focus on not rolling her underneath him. One touch, and he was a goner.

Ariel made a whistling sound and shook her head. "This is impressive."

"Glad you think so." Thaus grabbed her hand—gently, slowly—and directed her to rub him in an up-and-down motion that had his cock practically leaking with need. "Feels good."

"I would hope so." Ariel kept rubbing, kept teasing,

and Thaus kept enjoying every stroke. Eventually, though, he had to stop her.

"What's wrong?"

"You're going to make me come."

Ariel looked as if he'd spoken in another language. "Yeah?"

But Thaus had plans, and those plans needed time and care to come to fruition.

"I don't want to come like this." He pulled her hand to his lips, kissing the back before pulling her closer. "When you're ready, I won't stop you. But you have to go first. That's my one rule."

"You're serious?"

"Completely."

Ariel stared at him for a long moment, obviously surprised by his simple declaration. And when she spoke, when she finally opened her mouth to grace him with her words, it was with a smile on her face.

"You are amazing, Dire Thaus."

"As are you, Doctor Ariel. As are you. Now, rest with me for a while."

"Seriously?"

"Yeah. I think it's what we both need." Thaus closed his eyes and curled his body around his mate, feeling her warmth beside him. Listening to her breaths slow as she relaxed into the position. He rested and let the bond tying them together strengthen. Legs and arms tightened, bodies inched closer, until they were one heap in the middle of a very large mattress. A calm, happy heap.

And as Ariel slept safe and secure in his hold, Thaus plotted. He was in heaven, but hell was coming for them. A hell he'd have to fight to the death to keep his angel safe. And he would. Ariel was his, and there was no way he would ever let anyone take her from him.

The feeling of being watched woke Thaus from a sound and restful sleep. He had no idea how much time had passed, only that it was still dark outside and his mate was sitting up and staring down at him with a peculiar expression on her face.

"What?" he asked. He rubbed a hand up the side of her leg, not the top. Needing to touch but not wanting to startle her.

"Do you feel it?" When he didn't answer—because he had no idea if she meant his hand or something else—she tried again. "The bond. Do you feel the pull through the mating bond between us?"

Thaus focused inward, seeking out the connection. It was there, a deep, pulling to be near her. A pulse of lust encouraging him to claim her. A connection still so new, so fragile. So perfect. "I do."

"Me too. And I like it."

Thaus didn't reply. He simply sat with her as she worked out whatever was going on in her head. Waiting to know what it was she needed so badly that she'd woken from her sleep.

"Thaus?" Ariel rose to her knees and turned so she was facing the headboard. And him.

"Yeah?"

"I'm ready." His mate took a deep breath and sat up straighter; she even raised her chin as if about to battle something. Or someone.

But he refused to assume what she intended to be ready for. "For what?"

Ariel took a deep breath and pushed him. Literally shoving until he lay flat on his back. "I'm ready to complete our bond—to share mating bites with you. But I need to do this my way. I can't handle…"

She shook her head, and Thaus' heart broke for her. The fear in her eyes, the determination she had to muster simply to give in to what her body wanted. It killed him. The fuckers who did this, who dampened her confidence and spirit, deserved to be brought back from the dead and ripped apart again. Repeatedly.

But it was her shaky hands landing on his chest that pushed him over the edge.

"Hey." Thaus sat up and reached for her with slow, steady movements. "Nothing has to happen. I told you we could wait."

"You're going to fight the Glaxious pack." Ariel shook her head and curled into him, letting him rub his hands over her hips and thighs. And when she sighed and pressed her forehead against his chest, sitting beside him with their bodies pressed together, he closed his eyes and growled hard. Her skin, her scent, her warmth…it all worked together to undermine his resistance. The moment was so strong, so normal, Thaus could barely think, let alone speak. But he got out the one word he needed to so the conversation could continue, even as his cock wept for the woman.

"So?"

"So… You might die."

Ah, that helped clarify things. He huffed and shook his head even as he gripped her hips a little tighter. Risked pulling her a bit closer. "Not happening."

"How do you know?"

"I'm that good."

She laughed, sitting up once more so she could smile at him. And smack his shoulder. "Braggart."

But her words only portrayed a drop of what was really happening inside her. He could see it in her eyes, sense it in the emotions and energy she gave off. Ariel worried, and that wasn't something to use to kick off their physical relationship. He wanted her to want him, to desire him, to crave him…but not because she might lose him.

Thaus trailed a hand up her waist and sternum, skirting her breasts and pausing at her collarbone. "May I?"

Ariel stared at him for a moment, her big, dark eyes a theater playing every emotion. Lust, fear, desire, anger, need, panic…all there. All tearing him up inside as he saw what they were doing to her. How they weighed on her. And when she nodded, when she showed that strength he knew she had, he could only smile.

"I won't die because I have too much to live for." He cupped the side of her face, rubbing his thumb over her cheek.

Ariel closed her eyes and sighed, leaning into his touch. "I still worry."

"I know, but I'll be fine. My brothers and I are excellent at what we do. We aren't legendary without reason."

"Could be a pop-culture phenomenon. The Dire Wolves could be the shifter equivalent of Bigfoot to humans."

What the… "No."

"No?"

"No. We're not like Bigfoot."

"Too bad. Bigfoot is a great legend." Ariel laughed and lay against his chest before pushing him onto his back once more. She sprawled over him, creating a puppy pile of just the two of them. Thaus enjoyed the snuggling a lot, more than he cared to admit. He liked that she let him run his hand down her hair and back, too. But he needed direction from her, needed to know what she had planned so he could react accordingly. Her PTSD meant he needed to act with purpose and care, and not knowing what she wanted when they were both naked and alone was about as careless as he could get.

He would never be careless with her. "What's your goal here, Ariel?"

She was silent for a long time, but she finally whispered, "We have to have sex to exchange bites."

But the words sounded false, disconnected in a way, and he hated the tone of her voice. "Not necessarily. We could just exchange bites cold if you're set on that action."

"Cold?"

Thaus shrugged, staring at the ceiling and willing himself to stay perfectly still as his naked mate rubbed a pattern across his chest with her fingertips. *Heaven and hell, heaven and hell.*

"Might hurt more, but no one ever said you have to be having sex. It was just...one of the benefits."

Ariel laughed again, and Thaus groaned. The pressure of her against him, her body wiggling the way it was, didn't help his situation. He tried to keep his hard cock away from her, but there was almost no way to do that when she was on top of him. He shifted to the side a little, moved his hips over to give her more distance from it. But instead of letting him go, she moved the same way he did, and she rolled almost right on top of him. Trapping his cock between his stomach and her hips. And as much as he liked the position—loved it, loved the pressure and the heat—he had to move away. Somehow.

"Sorry." He rocked his hips back, trying to push them farther into the mattress. An awkward and uncomfortable position for sure. Ariel sighed and dropped her forehead to his chest.

"You're apologizing for being hard."

The ceiling gave him no answers on how to answer that one. "Sort of."

"I hate that." She looked up at him. "I hate that I'm so broken."

"You're not broken, just cracked a little. Totally repairable."

"Is that what you're doing? Repairing me?"

Thaus curled forward, enveloping her in his arms and legs, watching to make sure he didn't push her too hard. "No, I'm trying to be a good mate and take care of you in whatever way you need. Right now, you're struggling between your fears and the call of the mating bond. I'm trying to help you find the balance you're comfortable with."

Ariel stared at him for a long moment, and the tension between them grew. Pulling them closer as if they were magnets. Setting them up to crash together when resistance grew too hard. Thaus could only hope she surrendered first.

And maybe she did, in her own way. "I know they're sort of the traditional positions, but I'm terrified you'll try to climb on top of me—front or back—and I'll freak out."

Thaus didn't know whether to be turned on or off. The vulnerability of his mate left him reeling. By the gods, his woman was so strong. He pushed a lock of hair behind her ear and rested his fingers along her neck. Holding loosely, supporting with everything he had.

"Won't happen—the climbing on top on my part—I would never push you like that. You have all the control here."

Ariel huffed and growled. In an act of bravery the likes of which he'd never seen, she sat up and swung a leg over him. Straddling his hips. Putting herself in a position to... ride him?

"And this, me being on top, wouldn't bother you?"

Such a loaded question. As an Alpha-minded animal, of course, it bothered him. His wolf refused to submit to anyone, refused to take on a posture of submission. But this was his mate, his female. He would do anything for her. The man in him was fine with the idea of her on top. He quite enjoyed it, really. But his wolf liked a bit more control.

Still, he shrugged. "Not sure. Never done this before."

"No?"

"My wolf is too strong. He can't decide if having his naked mate ride him is the best thing ever or if he should throw you off and prove his dominance. The man, though…I'm good with letting you do all the work."

Another laugh from his mate, this time while his cock was happily ensconced between the two of them. The vibration made him moan, made the tingles of pleasure shoot up his spine in a way that caused his claws to come out. He reached for her thighs on instinct—wanting to hold her, rock her, set a pace for more—but thankfully stopped himself at the last moment.

"Fuck," he hissed, a sound like a whine bubbling up from his chest as he gripped the sheets. "This is going to be hard."

"Already is." Ariel rocked just as he'd wanted her to, nearly killing him with the heat and the wet and the motherfucking pressure.

"Not what I meant, baby."

"I know." She leaned down for a kiss, stealing his breath with her lips before rolling back up and pulling another deep groan from him. "Hang on to the headboard."

"What?"

Ariel nodded up the mattress. Thaus tilted his head back, following her gesture. The bed was a solid wood monstrosity, stable and strong, with a decorative iron panel Mammon had designed for him. Thick, solid metal bars woven together with large gaps in between. The damn thing suddenly seemed less decorative and a lot more functional.

"Good plan." Thaus did as she suggested, wrapping his hands into the metal and gripping tightly. "You don't have to do a thing, baby. Remember that. We can figure out how to calm the mating imperative without sex."

Ariel frowned. "This is so not sexy."

He nearly jackknifed off the bed. "What?"

"This. You and me. I wanted it to be sexy, but it's almost clinical. Hold this, sit like this, give me a damned pep talk just so I can consider having actual sex." Ariel sighed and pushed him back down. "It's not sexy."

Yeah…no. "Baby, you're completely naked, straddling my hips, and sitting on my cock. It's the sexiest thing in the fucking world."

"Such a charmer." She leaned down to give him a kiss, a deep one. The first that held so much passion. One led to two, which led to three, which led to her tongue in his mouth as she rocked her hips over him. His cock was covered in her wetness, and his balls pulled tight to his body as he fought his release. As she fucked his mouth with her tongue and rolled that soft, wet pussy over him with every breath. Ariel was going to make him come before he ever even got inside her.

"Ariel," he hissed as she pressed back. Sitting up, she let her head fall and rolled her hips over him in a rhythm that made him shake. Made him want to grab. Made him weak. And she fucking moaned. "Oh, now *that's* fucking sexy. By the gods, I want to be inside you."

She moaned again, rising up to grasp the base of his cock. And then she sat back. Slowly. Taking him inside in the longest, most torturous slide in the history of the world.

Thaus knew he'd finally died.

"You feel so huge inside me." Ariel hummed a soft, smooth sound. Not quite moan, not quite growl. All kinds of sexy. "I mean, I knew you were big, but to actually *feel* it…"

Her moans almost killed him, almost threw him right over the edge. And the way she curled her shoulders and closed her eyes, how her jaw fell open in what looked like uncontrollable pleasure…she was going to ruin him. He had to fight to hold back his orgasm, had to bite his lip and think of other things like some sort of pubescent pup to keep from embarrassing himself and disappointing her. The metal panel creaked as he tightened his grip, as he fought the hardest battle of his life not to let go.

"Fuck, Ariel."

Ariel groaned and rocked her hips in slow, sensuous moves, taking more of him, working herself down his cock. "Oh, yes."

"That's it," he said as she rose up just to slide back down. Teasing him in a way. Killing him in another. "Just like that. You okay?"

"Good. So fucking good." And she was. Ariel moaned and groaned and rocked her little body over his until she was gasping and arching and clenching around him. Until he knew she was ready to come. Thaus lifted her with his final thrust, rolling her to their sides even as he kept hanging on to the headboard.

"What…" Ariel's eyes popped open, unfocused and dark. Thaus wanted to run a finger along the side of her face, wanted to wrap his arms around her as they moved into this segment of their mating. He wanted so many things, but he couldn't have them. Not yet. Maybe not ever. And that was truly okay with him.

"Mating bites?" Thaus kept his hips moving, his thrusts shallow. Ariel's head fell back as he dragged the base of himself over her clit. Interesting. The position had merit—he'd have to remember it.

"Yes. Please, yes."

Thaus had to close his eyes, had to slow his hips and focus hard on not coming for another ten seconds. Had to keep her riding that wave toward her own release, though. He slid a hand between them to tease her clit as he leaned over her, giving himself to her first. Offering.

"Go." He pressed down on her clit, harder than he would have if she wasn't already so close. She grunted and gasped, her body responding to his touch in the way he knew it would. A powerful orgasm rolling over her, making her shake.

"Thaus…"

"Go."

And she did. Her teeth slid into his neck in a bite that set off explosions within him. It took everything he had not to roll her over. Not to pull her underneath him and fuck her until they both saw stars. He fought that urge hard, focusing on the pleasure she'd given him, the needs laid out before him.

He focused on his own bite.

Legend had it that some pack women would give their mates bites in secret places. Legs, backsides, right above their cocks…someplace meant for that female alone. Thaus had never understood that compulsion. Part of the mating imperative was that every other fucker around would know the shifter had a mate. He wanted his bite visible to the world, wanted it to be a calling card of sorts. Ariel had bitten his neck—high enough that no shirt would ever cover it—and he wanted to return the favor.

Without pinning her, without even holding her in place, Thaus scented along her neck muscles until he found the perfect spot. Still thrusting, still rubbing her clit, still pushing them toward more and more, he leaned in. And he fucking gave his mate her claiming bite.

Explosions and fireworks and utter pleasure raced through him, her groans and screams as she came all over again adding to the moment. She was his. He was hers and she was his. Their bond was solidified, deeper and stronger than anything else. He would nurture it, cherish it, and help it grow. And no one would ever get between them. Period.

They collapsed in a heap of legs and skin, her on top of him in a way he found surprisingly erotic. His arm around her waist, her body lying across his chest, Thaus was as blissed out as he'd ever been before. There was nothing like his mate in his arms, and there was nothing that would stop him from keeping her safe.

Which was why he jumped up the way he did when he heard footsteps approaching.

"What's wrong?" Ariel asked, pulling the sheet up against her chest.

"My brothers are here." Jeans were enough. He didn't need the rest, but he took the time to search out Ariel's clothes because she'd need them. Every stitch.

"We knew that," Ariel said, still looking confused. "They were outside, right?"

Thaus tossed her clothes on the bed. "They're on patrol for the night. They wouldn't be at the cabin unless something was wrong. Especially not both of them."

It took her a second to register his words, but when she did, she was on her feet. He hurriedly helped Ariel into her clothes before pulling her with him into the living room. Hands grasped together, no looseness to his grip. He refused to let her go. Couldn't stand the thought of being separated from her for a second. Especially not if there was danger nearby.

"What's happening?" he asked as soon as Phego walked in.

"They're closer than we thought and coming up more of an eastern route." Phego stopped and sniffed, looking from Thaus to Ariel and back before shaking his head. Shit, they had to reek of sex and mating and each other. A thought that was oddly comforting to Thaus. Phego would need to deal.

"Got something to say, brother?" Thaus asked, pulling Ariel closer.

Phego didn't even look at her, which was probably his smartest move. "We saw them at the bottom of the valley on the northeast side."

"Fuck." Thaus hurried outside, dragging Ariel with him.

Mammon was waiting just off the porch. "If we blast the

whole thing instead of in sections, we can block them, but because of the vastness of the slide, our best route of escape would be west toward the ocean. Every human around will be trying to head south, and they'll be in our way. We can't risk exposure or collateral damage."

That was not the plan Thaus had intended on. "If we don't blow the ridge?"

"They'll be here in a few hours."

"We fight either way," Phego said.

"Why is having to run west a bad idea?" Ariel asked.

Thaus couldn't answer her, couldn't doubt her when everything was going to shit, but Phego could.

"Because of you."

Thaus' growl came without warning. "Phego—"

"No disrespect whatsoever, but you're what they're after and our weakest link. Without you here, running wouldn't really be part of the plan. It would be a last-ditch effort should those fuckers get too close, sure, but not a main option. Running toward the ocean limits our escape routes."

"I can run," Ariel said, standing up to the big, bad wolf before her.

But she didn't understand the dilemma, and Phego did. "Can you swim, though? Can you leap off a cliff to avoid the rocks below and swim through the rough into deeper water?"

Ariel stared, not answering. Probably not having thought about the geography of the area.

"I can't swim," she finally whispered, sounding so scared and lost. Thaus hated that voice.

Phego sighed, looking as upset by the tone in Ariel's voice as Thaus felt. "I say we blow the ridge and get ready to run west if need be."

"Ooh Rah," Mammon grunted. "Let's blow some shit up."

Thaus tugged Ariel closer, keeping to the one-arm hold she seemed to be okay with. "You need to hole up inside.

I know you don't want to be left out, but I have to make a fuckton of bombs go off in just the right sequence, which takes time. I need to know you're safe."

She sighed but rose up to drop a quick kiss to his lips. "Fine. But next time, I get to blow shit up, too."

There wouldn't be a next time—he'd make sure she was never in danger like this again. But she didn't need to know that. "Understood."

Seventeen

riel had thought she'd fought back her demons and earned a bit of peace, but she'd been utterly and totally wrong. It had taken less than three minutes of the Dire Wolves planning for the hammer to fall. Thaus needed to go with Mammon to set up the blast site. He'd obviously struggled with the decision, so she'd made it easier with a smile and an *I'll be fine* and a *Hurry back*. He ended up buying her lies, kissing her forehead and rushing out the door as she fought to control the panic attack she could feel building, which meant she was left alone with Phego. A man who scared her more than the rest.

Perfect.

"Are you hungry?"

Ariel jumped and spun, tearing her gaze away from the door Thaus had left through to focus on the man trying to be nice. She was a mess.

"Uh, no. Not at all."

Phego frowned and gestured toward the kitchen. "I'm going to eat. You don't mind?"

"No. Please do."

He left her in the living room area of the open floor plan cabin so he could pull some supplies from the pantry. She could feel his eyes on her now and again, but she didn't react. Instead, she stood and stared at the door, willing herself to stay calm. To not panic. To focus on her breathing so as not to upset Thaus through their bond.

But Phego had other ideas. "You're number four, you know."

"Four what?"

"Mates."

If her heart could have crashed through the floor, it would have. Had Thaus had other mates? She'd never heard of a shifter being gifted more than one fated mate, but Dire Wolves lived a long time. It could be possible. As much as she would hope such a thing would be irrelevant to her current situation, that wasn't the case. Anger and jealousy bubbled up within her, almost overriding her fears.

"Four?" She cocked her head, regarding the shifter uneasily. "How'd they die?"

Phego growled, his eyes wide and his hand frozen in midair holding a huge butcher knife. "What?"

"Thaus' mates. How did they—"

"No, no, not Thaus." Phego laughed and shook his head as he went back to chopping up…something. "You're his one and only. I meant you're the fourth Dire Wolf mate. The fourth female brought into our pack."

"Oh." Four men mated out of seven after a millennia…those odds were slightly sad. "Where are the rest?"

"Bez and Sariel live in Texas. They're in Fort Worth right now with Mammon's mate, Charmeine. He wouldn't have come if he'd had to leave her alone. And Levi and Amy live in North Carolina."

"Your pack is spread out?"

"Yeah. We all choose our homes, you know? Wherever we feel comfortable."

The scientist in her was intrigued by this lifestyle as it went against everything most wolves cherished. The newly mated woman in her was more cautious about the whole idea. Live apart from pack? How did that work?

"And that doesn't strain the pack dynamic?"

Phego huffed an almost sarcastic laugh. "We've been together for centuries upon centuries...nothing strains that."

He gave her a look that seemed to say *not even you*, which only made her feel worse. Ariel hadn't thought about where she and Thaus would live once the Glaxious pack issue was taken care of, but apparently, it could be anywhere. So long as he was accessible to his pack for jobs. Would he want to move south to be with the two couples there? Did he have a place he saw as his home? He'd mentioned the cabin being his den, but she had no idea if he meant that as temporary or permanent. Funny, as bad as things were, she didn't want to leave the little house. Thaus and she'd created memories in this cabin, had started their mating here. She wanted to stay right where they were.

"You know you're safe, right?"

Ariel startled, refocusing on Phego who stood staring at her. Knife nowhere to be seen. "What?"

"You're safe with us. Any one of us." He sighed and shook his head. "Thaus is a brother, which makes you family. We'd never let anything happen to you."

"I...okay." But she didn't feel safe. Or maybe she didn't feel settled. Without Thaus by her side, there was a staticky sensation to her thoughts. Something rough and hard to decipher. Something she wanted to get rid of so she could concentrate once more.

"You lucked out. He's the best of us all. Loyal to the core," Phego said as he sat down to eat his meal.

But the food didn't matter. Not when his voice carried so much emotion. "You care for him."

He took a bite, chewing and swallowing as he seemed to think over her words. "I care for all my brothers and would die for any one of them, but Thaus is exemplary. I'd do anything for him because I know he'd do the same for us."

Ariel wanted to say something back, but her senses fired at that moment and propelled her toward the door. She could sense Thaus coming closer, could feel him through the mating bond. He was returning to her, and she couldn't wait.

Ariel was almost to the door when it flew open, and Thaus came storming in. He appeared like a man possessed, as if he'd lost something precious and was looking tirelessly for it. And when he saw her, when his eyes met hers, he growled. Precious thing…found.

She was in his gentle hold in a heartbeat, completely surrounded by him before she could take a breath. With his arms holding her off the floor, she wrapped her legs around his hips and held on tight. Needing him just as much as he seemed to need her. Sending him her own relief and need and desire as he flooded their bond with his.

"Yeah," Phego said with a sarcastic lilt to the word. "We'll be watching for the Glaxious pack outside."

He and Mammon shuffled past, but Ariel didn't care. Her mate was back, safe and sound in her arms once more. And she needed him.

"How long?" Ariel asked when the door closed behind the other Dires.

Thaus growled and pulled her tighter, nuzzling into her neck. Scenting her. "An hour or so, mate."

By the gods, did she love hearing him call her that. "Plenty of time."

Ariel bit his jaw and rocked against where he was already so hard for her, letting her desire be known. He set her on her feet and pressed his lips to hers, kissing her deeply. Fucking her mouth the way she wanted him to do elsewhere. The two stumbled to the bedroom, clothes torn off as they went, no care given to things like doors and locks and delicate skin. Scratches formed, lips were bitten, and fingers probably caused bruises as they grappled to get naked, but she didn't care. Let them both come out bloody and battered. It would be in the best way.

She was still wearing her panties when she finally pushed him onto the mattress. His jeans were around his ankles still, but she didn't bother with them. She needed. Wanted. Craved. And he didn't have to be naked for her to take.

Needful and unable to wait another second, Ariel climbed on top of him just as he grabbed that beloved headboard. She pulled the cotton fabric covering her pussy to one side and lined him up, sinking down with a quiet moan. But it wasn't quite enough.

"I want to be stronger," she said, rocking as she stretched to take him in. "Need to get better."

"You're pretty fucking perfect as you are," Thaus said with a groan.

"No, not that." She leaned down and pressed her lips to his, still rocking, licking across his lips in a way that almost seemed obscene. "I want to get better so you can be on top, my mate. I want to feel your weight on me."

"Fuck, baby." The headboard creaked as he pulled, but Ariel didn't want that. She didn't need safe or free at that moment. She wanted to be held by him. Only him.

"Put them on me."

Thaus frowned, slowing his own movements as he stared up at her. "Are you sure?"

Ariel gave the thought the time it deserved, but in the end, she nodded. The idea intrigued her, made her pussy wetter, exciting her to the point of pain. The bond to her mate reassured her that he had no intentions of hurting her. She knew that in a way, but the backup was nice. The surety that came from feeling such a connection a gift. She could be with him without fear…at least in some ways.

"Please. I trust you." And she did, which was something she hadn't fully expected to happen so soon. Thaus seemed to realize that. He moved his arms slowly, releasing the headboard almost one finger at a time. When he was finally free, he lowered his arms and grabbed her hips gently, not controlling, not pushing. Just…holding. Touching.

And it felt good.

"Harder," she gasped as she slid a hand to her pussy to press against her clit. Thaus groaned, his eyes locked on that hand. His fingers digging deeper into her thighs. The two rocked and thrust and groaned their way through their orgasms, both crashing within seconds of the other. Thaus arched almost off the bed, snarling through his teeth as her pussy clenched around him. Ariel came a second time, Thaus' pleasure pulsing through their bond throwing her over the edge one more time. A definite benefit to the whole mated-feeling bond thing.

"Baby," Thaus whispered, pulling her into a deep and delicious kiss. His hand on her hip, hers on his chest. It almost felt normal. Expected. No fear or panic, no visions of terror or anxiety blackouts. This was Ariel and her mate, and the moment was more beautiful than she could have imagined.

"We're almost there," she whispered, smiling down at the man who brought her so much joy. "You're putting me back together, and we're almost there."

Thaus furrowed his brow and leaned up for anther sweet kiss. "You're putting yourself together. I'm just holding the glue as you do."

They curled up together, one big pile of tangled limbs and sweaty skin. And as Ariel rested, as she prepared herself for what she knew was to come, she wondered if that was true. Had she made all the repairs herself? Or had Thaus pushed her with his patience and support? She might never know, the only way to be sure being to break the mating bond. Something she didn't want.

Something that brought back every ounce of anxiety she'd ever lived with.

Eighteen

The wind on top of the north ridge blew through Thaus' fur, bringing with it the scent of the bastards below him. For almost an hour, he sat and watched as the large wolves—the ones who weren't true wolves at all but shifters—picked their way up the rocky slope. Inching closer all the time. On target to reach the cabin as if they knew where it was. The more he watched, the more he saw how direct their path was, the more he knew how much trouble Ariel was in. And the more his fury grew.

Phego, back from a run along the western trail to evaluate the pacing of the intruders, crept through the trees and joined him on the overlook. Thaus shifted human when his Dire brother did, the two crouching behind a sliver of rock, still watching. Still waiting.

"They're climbing slow but on a straight trajectory," Phego whispered with his brow furrowed. "Is that the way you originally came up the mountain?"

"No." Thaus stared hard, wanting every single one of the fuckers below dead. "They know where they're going."

"How?"

"Either they have some sort of sense for her, which I doubt as she has no true connection to the Kwauhl pack, or…"

His growl cut him off, the sound too strong to hold back.

"I'm not following," Phego said. "If there's no pack connection, then how do they know where to go without tracking you two? It's not like any of us told them where you'd be."

"They're tracking her."

"But you just said—"

Thaus slammed his fist into the boulder, snarling violently as pieces fell together in his mind. "They know where we are even though they shouldn't, and they're not following any residual scent trail."

Phego's eyes went wide. "By the gods. They fucking chipped her."

By the gods was right. Though Thaus hadn't shared her history with the other Dires, he knew enough of it to have a feeling for what had happened to her. Which meant pieces of history were about to become current events.

"She refuses to be touched," Thaus said, his brain working through a pattern he didn't want to make sense of. But he would…he had to. "She's terrified of being held down. She was kidnapped and held against her will, but she escaped. She ran from them and made it pretty far, but then Glaxious brought up some centuries-old contract out of the blue after she joined the neighboring pack."

Phego's snarl joined his own. "Convenient, no?"

"No. Planned." Thaus shook off as much of his rage as he could, focusing hard on what he could do for Ariel's safety and not what he knew had to be true. If he thought about that… if he let himself truly consider what must be, he'd knock down the whole mountain in revenge.

But he needed to tell Phego.

"The kidnappers microchipped her like a fucking dog, and Glaxious knows it."

Phego was silent for a moment, watching the wolves below. "Which means the other Omegas could be chipped as well."

Thaus' heart jumped, the damned thing missing a beat as that reality washed over him. He'd been so concerned about Ariel that he hadn't considered the others. The Dires had joked for years about being chipped, as Deus, their tech genius, had tracked them via their cell phones. But true microchipping, placing a piece of equipment under the skin of a shifter without their knowledge, was universally thought of as disgusting. It removed a person's ability to run, to hide, to have free will over their location. It was simply something that wasn't done in any form.

Except by the bastards who'd taken Ariel, apparently.

There would be other Omegas with chips. Thaus didn't doubt that for a second. "We need to let Blasius know, and we need to kill these fuckers—especially their Alpha—so they don't go pulling up the next Omega who happens to be close enough to challenge for."

"We'll need Deus and Doc Shadow from the Feral Breed to look Ariel over," Phego said.

Thaus couldn't even picture that possibility. "She'll hate that. She won't want to be touched."

"You're her mate—you can stay with her and try to keep her calm. But if she's chipped, you have to get that thing out. Who knows if there are more packs like Glaxious with connections to the bastards who stole the shewolves? They could come back for her at any time. Removing that chip has to take priority."

Thaus knew that was true, but he was too locked into the past to really give the future much of his attention. Too stuck in the guilt eating him up inside. "I thought we took care of the Omegas."

"We did," Phego said with a growl. "We tracked down every fucking one. How this pack managed to figure out about chips we knew nothing about is beyond me, but we'll fix it. We will make sure those women are all safe. Starting by burying every one of these motherfuckers in a wall of mud and rock."

"We'd better. My mate's life depends on it."

Nineteen

"How'd you get stuck with babysitting duty this time?"

Ariel paced the kitchen, staying far away from Thaus' packmate, Mammon. It wasn't that she didn't trust him, she just didn't know him.

Okay, fine. She didn't trust him. She wanted to because he was with Thaus, but that wasn't happening. He was a big, scary, wolf shifter with shoulders the size of a small car. She had a right to be a little wary.

"Babysitting?" Mammon scoffed. "I consider it hanging out with my new pack sister. So, tell me, Ariel, how'd you end up mated to tall, dark, and dangerous out there?"

Ariel huffed a laugh. "He came rolling into a negotiation over who got to own me, and the fates took over."

Mammon growled low. "No one owns you. We'll make damn sure of it."

If she'd been a little younger, she might have blushed. "Thanks."

"No problem." He glanced down at his phone and

smiled. The look worked for him, made him seem so much... smaller? No, not smaller. Less intimidating. A smiling Mammon was a not-so-scary Mammon.

"News from the guys?" Ariel doubted it, but she hoped. She hoped hard. She missed Thaus and worried about him out there. She wanted this attack over so they could start a life together. They hadn't even taken the time to discuss where they'd go after this.

"Huh?" Mammon glanced up as his phone vibrated in his hand. "Oh no. My mate. She texts me sometimes."

"Texts or sexts?"

His eyebrow went up in a cocky sort of way. "Wouldn't you like to know?"

"Not really. What I would like to know is what's happening out there."

"Nothing."

"How do you know?"

Mammon shrugged, still looking at his phone. "Because I know."

But Ariel wasn't convinced. "What if the explosives went off early?"

He snorted. "Not possible."

"You act like you know."

"I do know."

"How?"

"Trust me, sweetheart," Mammon said as he typed on his phone again. "When that thing blows, you'll know. The whole damn mountain will know. Thaus isn't going for subtle."

"I need more data than that." And that right there was the trouble with being so analytical. Ariel needed information. Processes. That was her job. Dissect data, eliminate possibilities until a diagnosis could be reached, treat as specified. With Thaus out in the woods and not feeding her information about what he saw, she couldn't decide how bad things were. But she felt him—his worry, his fear, his fury. The man was on edge, and she had no clear understanding of the reason why.

Ugh, so frustrating.

The sound of Mammon's phone vibrating again grated on her nerves. "How can you just sit there and text?"

"Because I know they're doing what they need to. My job is to chill until shit kicks off. And my mate wants to talk to me."

"So we do nothing."

"Yep," he said, popping the P like some sort of adolescent. "Until we're needed."

"And we'll know that how?"

"You'll just know."

Ariel was about ready to throw a book at his head. "Can you put the damned phone down? I don't know how I'll just magically know when—"

The cabin shook with what felt like the power of a huge earthquake. Plates rattled, cabinet doors popped open, and Ariel swayed on her feet. The entirety of the earth seemed to move beneath her. Mammon simply smiled and tucked his phone into his pocket as he rose to his feet.

"Told ya we'd know."

Ariel could only stare, her heart racing in her chest. That was what they'd been waiting for? That didn't feel like a small explosion to start a mudslide—that felt as if the world was ending all around them.

But before she could say a word, Mammon's eyes darted to something behind her, and a roar sounded from his chest. He was across the room in a heartbeat, his hands rough and hard as he grabbed her. As he yanked her right off her feet.

Visions swirled, blocking out the reality she knew had to be there. Pictures of metal tables and chains, wires suspending women from the ceiling, and tools she couldn't even focus on for fear of throwing up. She was back there. Back in that place that had tried to steal her soul.

She was lost.

The world spun as she tried to scream, but it was no use. Panic set in, lights faded, and the sound of her own heart pounding drowned her.

And then the front door exploded inward.

Twenty

"Ready?"

Phego nodded, silent and mostly still as he watched over the drop zone. Thaus had set the charges, had planned and plotted and meticulously mapped out each and every one so he could loosen as much of the underlying support as possible with one blast. Every bomb linked to the detonator he held, the life of every wolf below also in his hand.

"Going live." Thaus closed his eyes and said a silent prayer that the forest would someday forgive him, and then he entered the detonation code.

One second…

Two seconds…

Three—

The explosion ripped through the valley below, a cloud of dust and debris shooting into the air from above them. Phego watched the wall of rock begin to break and slide, but Thaus focused lower. He kept his eyes glued on the team that had been making their way up the slope. The ones who didn't have time to get out of the way.

Thaus focused on his victims.

But when boulders began slamming into the first wolves on the hill, Thaus' show ended. He'd done what he needed to, and he had no regrets about that. He also didn't need to watch all those men die. He had a mate to protect.

The ground was still shaking, mud still falling down the mountain, when Thaus shifted to his wolf form and headed for the cabin. There was nothing left to do but wait for the dust to settle before the second part of the operation could begin. The retrieval. But he wanted to be with Ariel before he started the long and arduous task of picking through the rubble to make sure every wolf, every shifter that had been coming for her, was dead. He would not leave her open for another attack.

Over rocks and fallen trees, he ran with Phego right beside him. His Dire brother was as steady and sure as ever, keeping up without complaint. Phego hadn't questioned Thaus' need to be done, hadn't bothered trying to convince him to hit the hill for pre-stage recon before returning to the little cabin. He probably already knew Thaus would have refused. All Thaus could think about, all he cared about in that moment, was Ariel.

He needed to be by her side.

The two wolves were halfway back to the cabin when a sudden bolt of fear almost took Thaus to his knees. It damn near sent him sprawling, but Thaus fought it back. That fear wasn't his own; it wasn't from inside his mind or heart. The fear was pure Ariel.

As he regained his footing, Thaus let loose a roar that shook the treetops and lengthened his stride. There was no warning, no feeling of small fear or more worry than what he'd become accustomed to as her base level of him not beside her. No. This was sudden, sharp, and strong…like one of her panic attacks but cranked up to a level ten. Whatever had happened, he needed to fix it. He needed to get to Ariel.

And he would kill Mammon if his brother wasn't protecting her.

Twenty-one

*P*anic attacks were a bitch. Ariel had dealt with them before—lost moments and blackouts as her thoughts got locked away somewhere inside her mind for safekeeping, the pressure on her chest making her feel as if she couldn't breathe, the pounding of her heart in her ears to the point that she couldn't hear anything else. She'd suffered through them hundreds of times at that point, but she'd never had one clear up so fast. One second, she was lost in the fear that Mammon's touch incited. In the next, she was spinning for the door that had just shattered, ready to fight.

She was not going back to the chains.

Mammon's growl followed her as she moved slightly behind him. She wasn't stupid—the man was six foot six of solid muscle. Who wouldn't let him take the lead?

Three shifters raced inside, all heading straight for Mammon. Ariel kept her eyes on the door, though. She still wasn't stupid—those three were the distraction. The real danger was on its way.

And it arrived in the form of Alpha Chilton.

"We meet again, Omega."

She crept along the length of the island, staying out of the way of Mammon's fight but not moving toward the asshole at the door.

"What? You no longer know how to speak?" Chilton's arrogant smirk sent a chill down her spine, but she stayed focused and as calm as she could be considering the situation.

"I don't need to talk to you," she said, eyeing the door behind him and judging it too hard to get to with him in the way.

"Oh, but you do. You have a choice to make. See, your mate is in a lot of danger."

That pulled her up short, even as her brain told her it was probably a lie. "What kind of danger?"

"The kind that breaks that mating bond and sends him to the hell he belongs in," Chilton said, his words coming out with a growl. "You have five seconds to come with me, or my men kill him."

Ariel huffed a laugh. "Thaus already set off the mudslide. Your team is dead."

"What…did you think I only brought the one team? Oh, right… None of you knew about the ones on the south slope." He tapped a finger to his chin. "How hard do you think it was to send a third group on another trek up the eastern trails to surround those two men with the explosives? Your mate, Thaus…and his friend. What was his name again? Oh, right. He took his moniker from the demon Belphegor. You would know him as Phego."

The cold chill of surrender crept up her spine. She was too keyed up to feel Thaus through their mating bond, too frazzled even to reach for him. All she knew was that she'd dreaded him going out to those cliffs all day, and Chilton had just reminded her why. He likely had her mate penned in, and there was almost nothing she could do about it.

"Call them off," Ariel said, standing tall as Mammon tossed one of the shifters he was fighting across the room. She couldn't even think of them, though. Couldn't do anything to help Mammon at that moment. Her goal was to keep Thaus alive; nothing could deter her from that.

"Come with me now, and I'll make sure he lives"—Chilton's smile grew—"to make it back to the cabin."

"Not good enough."

He shrugged. "That's the best I can offer."

Ariel glanced toward Mammon. The man was practically pinned down by the other shifters, fighting his damnedest to get out of the pile. And still, even with two shifters trying hard to take him down, his eyes kept darting her way. Watching. Worrying.

She had become a serious distraction. She needed to buy the Dires some time.

"Your best sucks." Ariel took a deep breath and held her head high as she readied herself to fight back.

Chilton only smiled. "I'm so glad you said that."

With a whistle from the Alpha, four more men ran in the door. Mammon snarled and clawed at the floor, but he was too trapped to help. And Ariel…well, she wasn't fast enough to get out of the way. The four men grabbed her and yanked her toward the door, holding her arms to her sides and lifting her right off her feet. She was trapped. Helpless. Completely at their mercy.

And seriously pissed off.

But when she was thrown to the dirt in the front yard, that rage quickly melted into fear. Four more men stood along the tree line. Waiting for her, it seemed. Nine to one…she had no chance with those odds. And if Thaus made it back, if he reached them right then, she doubted even he could win in that fight.

"You've been busy," she said, gritting her teeth as one

of the shifters tied her hands behind her back. She choked back a sob and fought a wave of panicked dizziness when his hands grabbed her wrists, when his skin touched hers. She couldn't lose herself. Not right then. She had to stay focused and calm so she could figure out an escape plan. She was on her own in this one.

"I like to keep as many balls in the air as I can. Pack Alpha for Glaxious was only one." Chilton nodded to someone behind her.

"Move it," a harsh voice said as someone yanked her to her feet and pushed her forward. Ariel stumbled, almost falling. She couldn't fight back, and she couldn't shift. If she tried, she'd rip her shoulders to pieces, and that would take time to heal. Time she didn't have. So she went along with her kidnappers, and she held on to her sanity with every bit of strength she had left. She also pushed at her mating bond, but she was too keyed up, too close to panic, to know if there was anything coming back. Still, she tried. Because Thaus would come for her. He'd save her if she couldn't save herself. He'd never give up looking. She just needed to survive long enough for him to find her, which was something she had experience doing. The staying alive. The rescuing by someone else would be a first.

Two men half walked, half dragged her through the woods while Chilton and the rest of the wolves trailed them. The rocks bit into her bare feet and the branches from the trees whipped her in the face, but she didn't react. She refused to show a single sign of weakness. She was also too busy scoping out the land and looking for any advantage she could find.

But as they reached a precipice of stone that dropped at the sharpest angle she'd ever seen, Ariel was pretty sure her time was up. The sea below looked rough and deadly, the rock wall hard and impassable. And the trail leading in the direction they seemed to be headed? Too narrow to traverse. At least to her. Besides, even if she could survive the fall, she couldn't swim. She'd drown for sure.

"Keep moving. Unless you want to find out how cold that water is down there," one of the captors said. His leer chilled her spine but not as much as that potential fall.

"It's hard to balance." Ariel turned, offering her hands. They had to cut her free before they...

"Look how dumb," the man said. "She thinks we're going to make this easy on her."

Okay. So...balancing on a precipice without her arms or hands. Tricky. But at least they'd stopped touching her. She'd been in worse spots before. She just needed to calm down, breathe slowly, and not fall.

Oh, and not look down even for a second.

With her stomach in knots but her eyes locked on the point where the trail and the rock wall met, Ariel took her first step. And then her second. Not looking down. Not lifting her feet up more than she absolutely had to. She would survive this kidnapping. She had to.

It took the group far less time than she'd assumed to make it across the thin trail and around to the next plateau. Ariel could have sworn she held her breath the entire time, especially if the headache and churning stomach were any indication. No wonder the Dires had no idea the group had come up this way. That anyone would choose that particular path seemed ludicrous.

"Just a bit longer," Chilton said as he headed south along the cliff face. "Don't get scared now."

He pushed Ariel in front of him and kept them moving. This time, toward the drop-off. Ariel couldn't keep the fear back at the sight of the foamy water below. But as that burn of panic grew, so did something else. A comforting sensation of safety. A soft, pulsing connection to another person. Growing bigger, warmer, and closer with every second.

Thaus was coming.

Twenty-two

When he finally reached the cabin, Thaus stormed in and shifted right there in the kitchen. Ready to battle.

But he was too late.

The place was trashed. Glass on the floor, cabinets cracked and broken, and Mammon—bloodied and battered but refusing to back down—battling with three wolves in the living room. Phego jumped in to help right away, but Thaus took a look around instead, knowing his brothers could handle themselves just fine. The cabin wasn't that big, but still, he checked every room. Every closet. Even though he already knew he wouldn't find her.

Ariel was gone.

Thaus could sense her, though. Could feel the constant pulse of her fear. It created static through his brain and left his thoughts unfocused and scattered. He could sense her but not track her, feel her but not tell where she was. Her fear was so great, it obliterated the bond between them and left him scrambling to keep up. Or maybe it was his fear. He had no way to tell.

But Thaus didn't need to track her to know what had happened. Someone had targeted the cabin and snatched her. That was the only thing he could come up with. Someone not on that north mountain. Someone…

Someone who knew where she was and therefore could avoid the longer, tougher trek. Fuck, Chilton had tricked him. He'd sent a convoy up the northeast path as decoys, and Thaus had bought in to the ruse like an untried pup. He was going to slaughter that fucker.

Thaus rushed through the living room, ignoring the last few hits of a fight his brothers had won. He didn't need to be involved, didn't need to worry about the pawns Chilton left behind to keep his brother busy. They probably knew nothing of Chilton's plans and were therefore completely expendable. Thaus needed to find his mate. Immediately.

But when he reached the porch, he froze in utter confusion. She was everywhere and nowhere. North and south, east and west. His sense of her spread like a ripple in a pond, like an echo in a chamber, making it hard to find the epicenter. Making it almost impossible. And that fact nearly drove him to his knees.

"What happened?" Phego asked as he and Mammon rushed out to Thaus' side. Thaus didn't answer. He already knew, but he couldn't have forced the words out past his lips if he'd tried.

Mammon growled and wiped a trickle of blood off his forehead. "They snuck up the south side of the mountain. I didn't even hear them until they were at the door."

"And Ariel?"

Hearing her name was the break Thaus needed. "He tracked her."

"Who?" asked Phego, forcing Thaus to meet his eyes as he stood right in front of the Dire. "Who tracked her?"

Thaus released a growl that came from his very soul.

"Chilton. He'd been tracking her. He knew she was here, so he sent a group to make themselves seen on the north side. He and a handful of others came up the south side at a slower pace. You can still smell five, maybe six of them. He tricked us, and I fell for it."

"All this for some old fucking contract?" Phego asked.

No, not the contract. That didn't fit a damned thing that was happening. Thaus let his thoughts wander, remembering the pack and the packlands, the disarray and rotting structures. The feeling of being watched and the sense of a much larger pack than Chilton claimed as his own.

The fact that Ariel had escaped her captors...the only Omega he knew to do so without help.

The sense of hunters circling the Glaxious land.

Chilton.

And the contract.

"No," he said, trying to keep up with his thoughts. "This has nothing to do with the contract. Chilton didn't want to claim her as a mate. He wanted to hunt her, to chase her so he could prove he was better than she was. He and his real pack were involved in the Omega kidnappings, and they wanted to get to her because she found a way to escape. They brought out that old contract to make her run."

"But, why?" Mammon asked.

The answer slammed into Thaus like a truck without brakes, sending his stomach hurtling into his throat. "This isn't a contract negation or a mating. It's not even revenge for her turning Chilton down. This is a hunting party."

Thaus swallowed hard, holding back his need to shift. His overwhelming desire to race through the woods and strike down anyone he came across. "They're hunting the one who got away to prove a point."

"Motherfucker," Phego said, growling harshly. "Mammon, where's Ariel?"

"They snagged her a few minutes before you came in." Mammon met Thaus' glare, an apologetic and sincere expression in his eyes. "I swear, man. I jumped between them. I tried to get her out of their way, but she freaked when I grabbed her arm and almost ran right to them. I don't think she knew what was going on at that point."

Of course, she didn't. She needed safety and security, needed time to trust and find her comfort spot. She couldn't be grabbed or manhandled. Hell, he couldn't grab her hand without thinking about triggering her fears, and he was mated to her.

But he'd left her to deal with the explosives, and that had been his biggest mistake. Thaus should have long ago taught the other Dires how to wire the explosives so he wasn't the one who'd had to go. But he was the head of their armory, the weapons specialist for the Dires; he was the one who'd always monitored and stocked their supplies and knew how to use every one of them.

He'd failed his mate because he'd owned his job. A harsh lesson for the newly mated wolf.

"She's strong; she'll fight. But I need to get her back," Thaus said, and he started to run. Before he hit the south tree line, Mammon grabbed his arm. Thaus struck without thinking, almost knocking the other Dire down.

"Settle," Mammon screamed with a growl. "Take the time to feel her. Know where we're going before we start racing through the woods."

That was easier said than done, though. "I can't get a bead on her. She's too stuck in her head."

"Or you are." Mammon took a deep breath, imploring Thaus with every word. "Trust me, you'll feel her. Focus on that bond. Push past all the rest of the static around it, and reach for the thread connecting you. It's there, and you'll know where she is once you find it."

As much as he hated the waiting, Thaus knew Mammon was right. So he stilled his body and quieted his mind. And he searched for his mate. For her fear, for her pain. For her soul. He searched for minutes, standing completely still in the mountain breeze. He let the world go quiet, let the beast within go still, and he thought of nothing but the feel of connection to the woman he most wanted to find.

"West," he said the second he made contact. "They're heading for the ocean."

Phego was already headed that way. "Then let's go."

The three shifted to their wolf forms, Thaus grunting through the transition as his shoulder screamed in pain. It didn't stop him, though. He raced through the woods on four paws without a limp. He'd give in to the pain once he had his mate back.

Twelve paws beat into the forest floor and scrambled for purchase on the rocky ground. Their beasts were made for this sort of thing—were far more skilled and balanced on the terrain than their human counterparts. Going wolf would definitely be faster than staying on two feet, but Thaus could only hope it would be fast enough.

The drop-off ocean cliff came up faster than he'd expected, a solid, sheer slab of rock dropping straight down to the water below. From the sea, it looked as if a wall of stone had risen from the depths to block passage eastward. From the top, it looked as deadly as it truly was. And Ariel was up there.

Thaus followed her emotional trail almost to the edge of the cliff, then turned north. Closer, closer…he raced as hard as he could, knowing she needed him. Feeling her fear turn to panic and then terror. Worried he would be too late.

The Dires took a turn around a rock cropping, and finally, Thaus could see her down the path. On a flat piece of rocky land leading right to the edge of the world, a large

186 • ELLIS LEIGH

group of men stood surrounding her...one of them Chilton. Ariel was backed right up to the edge of the cliff, her chin up and her head back in a posture of defiance. Once more looking like the pissed off woman who'd stormed into the meeting hall back on Kwauhl packlands. His mate was fighting back.

But there were too many men between her and him, and that cliff was too close.

Thaus pushed harder, raced faster, the dread of the situation wrapping around him like a straitjacket. Knowing he was out of time. He was too far away, unable to reach her in time. He could sense her next step; saw it playing out in his mind. And still, he ran. Because it was Ariel, his mate, his angel. He'd promised to keep her safe, and he wouldn't fail her.

The men inched forward in concert, Chilton leading the way and obviously preaching at her about something. The what didn't matter because Thaus already understood the why. They were going to make her choose—live and go with them, or die and fall to her death. A clear decision for a woman with her history.

And still, he ran, knowing exactly which option she would choose.

Certain he was about to watch her die.

Twenty-three

As if she had called his name, three wolves appeared from the trail she'd just walked down. All three were of a massive size, larger than any other shifters she'd ever seen. And they were running straight for her.

All three Dires had made it.

"They're coming," one of her captors said.

The humans and wolves all turned to see, to watch the cavalry close in. To see a legend in motion.

"Shit, why are they so spotty?" one of the men asked.

Ariel almost grinned at his ignorance. Dire Wolves. The spots, the size... Anyone with a certain level of knowledge of wolf-shifter history would know what they were. True, they'd been thought to be extinct for centuries, and the old stories had long faded out of fashion, but she still knew. Still recognized them. Thaus had told her, but she'd recognized him for what he was the moment she saw his wolf that first time. And she was still amazed.

"You won't win against them," Ariel said as Chilton came around to her side.

"Oh, you stupid child. I already have. You see, I needed my pack destroyed so I could start over. Those fools knew too much and were getting too strong to hold off." Chilton's smile chilled her right down to her feet. "Your guards will be busy with my men for a while yet. It's time for us to go."

Ariel stood locked in place, though. "He'll come for me. He'll track me."

"You think I haven't already figured that out?" Chilton tsked then leaned in, whispering in her ear. "I know how to hide a mating bond so you can't be tracked. You'll be all mine."

Her stomach fell, and the fractures of panic inside her mind overtook her, spreading into canyons. He'd take her, and she'd be lost forever. What if she couldn't escape like last time? What if he figured out how to keep her contained?

What if the nightmares of her past were back to haunt her?

Ariel took a deep breath and stared at her mate as he raced toward her. Soon. That fight would happen in seconds. But he was still far away. So, so far. And he had to win against Chilton's enforcers once he reached the plateau. Three against…well, a lot, even though Chilton wasn't fighting. That would still take time, still require a patience she no longer had. That fight would give Chilton the chance to whisk her away and chain her up just as those bastards had done to her once before.

No.

She was on her own again. Her options were limited, but she'd choose the one that gave her the most control. The one that had a chance of a happy ending. If anyone could find her after what she was about to do, it was one of the Dire Wolves. But if they didn't, well…things could have been worse. So with another deep breath and one last, longing look for the man the fates had chosen for her, for the man who'd been so patient with her, the one she'd truly thought she could love, Ariel forced those canyons in her mind to seal closed. And she grabbed the reins of her fate.

"You don't get to own me," she said to Chilton. His eyebrows went up, confusion clear on his pointy rat face. But he was slow, too slow. He didn't see it coming, didn't think she'd do it. He'd never been backed so far into a corner that the only way out was destroying everything you were.

Ariel had, and she never would again.

Without another word, she turned and ran for the edge of the cliff.

Twenty-four

The scene played out in some sort of nightmare tempo. Thaus' legs grew heavy, almost mired down as if in quicksand, as Ariel looked his way one last time. As she peered straight at him for a moment. He understood what she was about to do before she did it, knew she was saying good-bye so she could play the only card she had left. And that fucker from Glaxious had no idea. Chilton had considered her wily but weak, which was wrong. No one came through the other side of what Ariel had without a war chest of strength. Even at her weakest, she would always be stronger than just about anyone else. That strength wasn't physical; it was a mental thing—a need to regain control. And Ariel was about to prove that to Chilton.

While Thaus watched, unable to make it to her in time.

The break was quick—faster than even Thaus had expected. One second, Ariel stood watching him. Saying good-bye with her eyes. The next, she was running. Chilton just stood in dumbfounded shock as Ariel spun and raced toward the drop-off. Probably unable to believe she would do such a thing. But Thaus knew her. He saw her fears and her battles and understood exactly what the threat was and why she was taking the option of the sea. Death to Ariel would be better than going anywhere with Chilton. He must have told her about the chemicals they'd used during the Omega kidnappings. The ones that had quieted a mating bond until the partner couldn't sense their mate. Until the kidnapped couldn't be found.

Ariel was terrified of being trapped forever in the hell she'd escaped from once, so she was choosing her only other option. Thaus didn't blame her; he just hoped he was fast enough to save her.

The scene of her jumping played out in slow motion— the push off from the edge Ariel managed even with her arms behind her back, how she seemed to deny the force of gravity as her feet left the ground, and the way she seemed almost relieved as she hovered for one brief moment in midair.

And then she fell out of sight.

Mammon chuffed once, a low, breathy sound that said more than human words ever could. Phego growled low, a constant sound that edged on a whine every few steps. Thaus understood them, though. He heard their fears. He felt their need to save her.

He knew they'd understand why he couldn't help them fight.

There wasn't even a pause in Thaus' stride, wasn't a moment where he worried about anything other than Ariel. He put his faith completely in his brothers to deal with the threat of the Glaxious pack and went after what he needed to. Thaus pushed himself faster, harder, stretched his stride longer. He raced for the edge of the cliff like his life depended on reaching it…because it did. And just as he hit the edge, just as he reached that asshole Alpha Chilton, he took care of the one piece of business he needed to that wasn't all about saving his mate from the waters below.

It was about saving her when he finally pulled her out.

One paw, four claws, and a wolf running at a high rate of speed could create enough damage to take a shifter out of commission for days. Thaus struck on the fly, never veering off course, never pausing. The blood spray from Chilton's wounds didn't even slow him down as he ran those last few feet. That would keep the man, the one responsible, out of commission while his brothers dealt with the enforcers. Chilton couldn't escape—he'd come after Ariel again, and Thaus wouldn't allow that. He would protect his mate.

When his paws hit the edge, when his claws curled around the final step of solid ground he had, Thaus pushed off hard. And he jumped right after her.

Thaus shifted in midair from wolf to his human form. The burn of his shoulder barely registered, though the stiffness in his arm certainly did. Still, he couldn't focus on that. He had a mate who couldn't swim about to hit a wall of water so choppy, even the rocks seemed fearful of it.

Needing more speed, Thaus purposely tucked his arms in and held his legs together to fight wind resistance. She was there, below him, still falling. He couldn't stop her, but he could aim for her. He could follow her into the swells.

So he did.

His heart jumped when she disappeared beneath the water, but he locked his eyes on that spot and let loose a roar that sent birds to the skies. He wouldn't lose her. Not after he'd finally found her.

When he hit the water, his first thought was cold, but then his instincts took over. He closed his eyes and held his breath, reaching for the one thing he cared about in that moment. The salty water swallowed him, the waves rolling him deeper immediately. There was little light and a hell of a lot of sound as the pressure sucked him deeper, making it impossible to see Ariel, to know where she'd gone. Burying his senses in nothing but water.

Still, Thaus pushed their bond to the max, seeking their connection in a way he hadn't before, needing it to be the driver through the dark, churning waters. He hit something hard, bouncing off it and losing some of his breath, but still, he sought her. Still, he fought the current and the rocks for her.

That bond succeeded, but so did Ariel, in her own way. As he focused on their bond, her hair floated into his hand as if by magic. The sensation of connection, of relief, was more than Thaus had ever experienced. He immediately went into action, yanking her up and into his arms so as not to lose her. He had no time to worry over if she'd freak out being touched, grabbed, or surrounded—this was life or death, and he'd do anything to save her.

Without thought, Thaus started paddling toward what he really hoped was the surface. He didn't have much time left. Already, his lungs burned and dark spots floated in his vision. Ariel was limp in his arms, seemingly unconscious. He needed air and so did his mate. Immediately.

So he swam toward the one spot of light in the sea of darkness, and he held on to his future.

His gasp when he broke through the water came out almost as a howl. He dragged Ariel above the water and let her head rest on his shoulder as he regained his bearings. It took two lungfuls to clear his head enough to start paddling away from the rock wall and toward an inlet that would take him to calmer waters. Thanks be to the fates for air, but death by being bludgeoned against the rocks wasn't exactly in his plans.

Saving his mate was.

"Ariel." Still kicking toward shore, he lifted her head so he could see her face. Pale skin, paler lips, and no independent movement confirmed his thought that she was unconscious, but that didn't deter Thaus. She'd come back to him. She had to. So he tilted her head back and breathed into her mouth. Twice. Three times.

"Don't give up now." He squeezed her closer, still fighting the pull of the ocean, and once again breathed for her. Against the waves, against the rocks, against the odds, he fought for her with every breath.

And he won.

Ariel came awake just as a huge wave took them back under for a moment. She gasped and coughed, choking on the water still pummeling them. Dropping underneath the waves for a second even as he held on to her. Thaus cursed and pulled her closer with one arm, using his other to direct them toward the smoother waters. There was nothing safe about where they were, nothing that guaranteed they'd make it out alive and unharmed. Nothing but his own determination. He'd almost lost her, and he wasn't about to live through that feeling again.

"Come on, baby," he called over the roar of the waves. "We're almost to the shallows."

"My hands." Ariel choked, coughing hard against him. "I can't—" She dipped below the surface for a second before Thaus could yank her back up. "They're tied. I can't break the cord around them."

Thaus cursed and reached behind her, finding the nylon tie with ease. He let his wolf come forward enough to extend one claw, then sliced the fucking thing.

"Better?" He held on to her elbow to give her room to find her balance in the water. But Ariel didn't seem to need the distance. She wrapped her arms and legs around his body and grabbed hold of him.

"This is better," she said, her voice shaky. But fuck, it sounded so good to his ears. "I was so scared for a second."

"Thank the fates, Ariel." Thaus held her tightly, fear of

her freaking out gone. He could only be thankful they'd made it as far as they had, even though they still weren't out of the worst of the waves just yet.

Thaus kept kicking toward the smoother shallows, edging around a rock cropping that seemed to block the worst of the waves. Still, the force of the water was too much at times, rolling them under every few minutes. Thaus kept a hold on Ariel, though. Not even easing his grip. His shoulder burned and his skin felt too tight in the cold water, but he fought through it. For her.

"Are you okay?" he asked as he finally swam into less rough water with Ariel clinging to his chest. How they hadn't gone under more, he had no idea. But he was thankful they'd made it out of the chop.

Ariel nodded against his shoulder, still hanging on to him like a life preserver, which he sort of was at the moment. "Yeah. Is Mammon?"

Thaus shook his head, letting his soaking wet hair spray them both. She'd almost drowned but was thinking about Mammon.

"You're worrying about Mammon right now?"

"He tried to help, but I freaked when he grabbed me. I was worried he wouldn't fight well because of it." His mate nuzzled his neck, kissing over the spot where her teeth had left a scar a mere few hours earlier. She was so brave, so unbelievably strong, and so ridiculous for worrying about Mammon when she'd jumped almost to her death.

"No, Mammon is fine." Thaus closed his eyes and kicked toward shore, toward where he sensed his Dire brothers, taking Ariel with him. "I'm pretty sure he's headed this way."

"How'd they get past all those shifters Chilton brought?"

Thaus grinned and nodded toward the rock wall. "Dire Wolves, remember? Legendary—and not like Bigfoot."

"Avast, ye mateys," Mammon yelled from a cliff edge

about halfway up the face of the rocks. "How're you two doing down there?"

Thaus growled, though to be honest, he was really happy to see the guy. His shoulder was on fire from the running, shifting, and swimming, and the fight to the shore wasn't over yet. As smooth as the water became in the shallows, that was only compared to the wildness beyond the rock outcropping protecting them. It was still a hard swim to shore. He'd be glad to get out of the water.

"Just fucking dandy. Want to point me in the best direction so we don't get pummeled against these rocks?"

Mammon pointed to Thaus' right. "That way looks easiest. And don't worry. I handled most of the pack, and Phego's got Chilton all taken care of. We'll snag the runners once we get the little mermaid down there to safety."

Ariel jerked, a sense of fear radiating from her. "Chilton's alive?"

Thaus could have snarled, but he was more afraid of scaring Ariel than not. Fucking Chilton deserved far more than he was about to get.

"Not for long." Thaus swam the two of them in the direction Mammon had indicated, trying not to wince whenever he had to use his bum arm. "Phego's our best information gatherer. If he's taking care of someone, it's to get the information we need before we dispose of him."

Ariel paddled along with him, obviously much more comfortable out of the rough waves of the open water. "You mean like torture?"

"It's a possibility."

"Why? What does he have that you need?"

Thaus grabbed hold of the rock ledge and pulled the two of them along the length of it. At that point, it was easier than swimming. Even his legs were tired.

"Chilton knew where you were, baby. He and his crew were tracking you, but not by scent."

Ariel's eyes went wide. "So…oh. They microchipped me when I was…"

Thaus hated the way her voice faded. "Yeah. When we get to Chicago, we'll have the docs check you over to see if they can find something that gave them that access."

The waves finally flattened out. There wasn't far to go, though Thaus still couldn't touch the bottom of the bay. Ariel was quiet as they crept along the rock wall, almost introspective.

"There will be more," she whispered as Thaus' foot finally hit rocky bottom. "The other Omegas. If there's something in me, they all need to be checked."

Thaus agreed, but before he could respond, there was something he wanted. Something he needed more than anything else. Unable to help himself, he grabbed Ariel and lifted her so her legs were once again wrapped around his waist. Before she could argue, he planted a kiss on her soft but cold lips. The adrenaline coursing through him ebbed, leaving him shaky and slightly off-kilter, but he had his mate in his arms. She survived, and that deserved to be celebrated. Even if they were still in the water. Ariel must have agreed because she fisted her hands in his hair and held him to her, letting him dominate her through the kiss. Their bond hummed, pulling their souls closer and strengthening their connection. Uniting them in a way Thaus had never experienced.

"We won't leave any of you unprotected," he gasped when they finally broke apart. "Especially not you."

She tucked her forehead against his and wrapped her arms around his neck, still breathing hard. Fuck, that was a good kiss. The tingle in his lips and feel of his mate safe in his hold left Thaus calm and confident, let him enjoy the feeling of her in his arms.

"You didn't freak when I grabbed you," he whispered as he walked them through the chest-deep water.

Ariel shrugged, still clinging to him. "I was too worried about drowning."

"You're still not freaking."

"Because it's you." She looked into his eyes, her smile filled with emotion. "I feel safe with you."

Nothing could have meant more to Thaus than those words from her. "Good. Because you are."

"Yo, swimmers," Mammon yelled. He stood on a flat patch of rock a few yards away, looking ready to jump into the water if needed. "Ready to leave the pool yet?"

Naked and filthy, Mammon held out his hand. Thaus walked the two of them over to the spot, not sure how to handle the extraction. There was no way Ariel would let his brother pull her out. He'd need to climb out first, then drag her himself, but he didn't want to leave her alone in the water. Couldn't bear the thought of her being in danger for a single second, especially as the depth was still probably a little too high for her to keep her nose above water.

"You ready to get out?" Thaus asked her, still holding on. Ariel smiled and nodded before turning to his brother. His friend. His family…and hers.

"Keep your junk out of my face, okay?" She reached for Mammon's hand, not even flinching when he grabbed hold of her and pulled.

"Pretty sure the only face I want near my junk is my mate's." Mammon helped Ariel to her feet, all while Thaus stood nearby. Stunned.

"What?" Ariel asked, probably noticing the stupor he'd fallen into.

"He touched you."

"Yeah?" She grinned, faking as if it was no big deal. "He's family, right? You said we're all pack. I'm safe with my pack."

"Ooh Rah," Mammon grunted before reaching for Thaus. "Your girl is a badass, brother."

"Don't I know it." Thaus slid his arms around his mate when he reached the rocky shelf, pulling her closer with as much care as he could before diving in for one deep, delicious kiss.

"What was that for?" Ariel whispered when he finally pulled away.

Thaus shook his head and chuckled. "For being brave. And mine."

Ariel grinned. "All yours for sure."

Epilogue

Thaus was ready to kill someone. Not a random someone—a particular someone. Two someones, really. One of his packmates and a Feral Breed member. Both of whom were causing his mate fear and pain.

Killing seemed like the right idea.

"Don't kill them," Phego said from where he stood leaning against the wall beside the door that led into the room where Thaus' mate was. Where he couldn't go.

"They'd deserve it."

"No, they wouldn't."

Thaus nearly whimpered as his bond to Ariel buzzed. "She's hurting."

"They need to remove something from inside of her." Phego cocked a grin. "Imagine how bad she'd going to hurt in a few months, and that's totally your fault."

Jackass. And yet, Thaus couldn't hold back the goofy grin Phego's words caused. He wasn't kidding—in a handful of months, Ariel would be in a lot more pain than she was right then. But he'd be beside her through everything, and at the end, they'd have something that would make it all worthwhile. A tiny, sweet-smelling something that would change their entire lives.

Still, that didn't mean Phego could get away with calling that detail out. "You're an asshole."

"Yup. And you're acting like an idiot. She's in the care of a medical professional and one of our brothers. Trust them to do their jobs."

Thaus growled and paced, pushing as much calm and love through the mating bond linking him to Ariel as he could. And feeling helpless.

They'd taken the fastest way to Chicago after the whole Chilton episode was over and the Glaxious pack destroyed, but they'd been stuck waiting at the mansion ever since. Deus had wanted to study Ariel, to see what sort of frequency the chip inside her used, and President Blasius wanted to make sure if anyone was tracking her, they knew she was under the protection of the NALB. All fine and good, except it had meant months spent at Merriweather Fields as they waited for the right time to remove the damned chip. But a blood test along the way revealed that the time had come before the team was ready.

No one wanted a pregnant Omega being tracked in any way, just in case.

"You think about where you're going to move?" Phego asked, still looking overly casual. Thaus didn't buy the slouch or the slow drawl to his words. He knew Phego was ready to take him to the floor if needed. Deus and Shadow had told the Dires to stay out of the room while they removed the chip, something about the blood of his mate possibly causing Thaus to lose control.

Fuckers.

"Ariel wants to go back to the cabin."

Phego chuckled. "The scene of the crime. I can see that."

"I'm not sure, though." Thaus groaned and ran his hands through his hair as he stared up at the harsh overhead lights.

"Why aren't you sure?"

"The microchip."

"It'll be gone. All the Omegas are being located and checked. No more chips."

"But we don't know who else knows about it."

"Chilton said he was the only one with the tracking hardware," Phego said, his eyes bright with a hate all the Dires felt in regards to the chipping of the Omegas. "I worked him over for three solid days before disposing of him, and that story never changed."

"I still don't trust he told the truth. He and his pack knew where she was. They had her tracked to that mountain. As much as I want to live in that same place, it's tainted now. Plus it's too far from others. We'd have no backup if—"

He couldn't finish, couldn't find the words. That *if* could be anything from unknown threats coming at them to more guys like Chilton looking for Ariel. He didn't need solitude anymore—not with his mate possibly in danger and a new baby on the way. He needed safety and security. He needed a pack.

But the Dire pack was spread out.

"You thinking of heading to Texas?" Phego asked, seeming to have read Thaus' mind. Typical.

"Fuck and no, but Ariel doesn't want to go as far east as Levi, either. Plus, the idea of Amy's family pack with all twelve of her unmated brothers being close freaks her out. She won't admit it, but I can tell."

"She's still nervous around strangers."

"Yeah." Thaus stared hard at the door, his stomach tying itself into knots. "Shadow is a stranger."

"Deus is with her," Phego said, though even he sounded worried. "He's pack. She's okay with our pack."

"True." Thaus sat in a chair and leaned against the wall. Ariel had grown closer to his brothers than he'd thought possible. Especially Phego. Those two were thick as thieves for some reason. "If you were me, where would you go?"

Phego shrugged. "Alaska."

"You must like snow."

"No, I like safety. And being around Luc is about as safe as I could imagine being."

The man had a point. The Dire they all thought of as Alpha was another level of dangerous. Thaus could see why Phego would choose to spend time with Luc, but he couldn't do that to Ariel. Pack or no, Luc would terrify her. He scared most people even without her sort of history.

Phego was quiet when he spoke next, reserved almost. "You could always come to Montana."

Thaus stared hard at his brother, not sure of how to take that kind of offer. Phego lived in Montana most of the year, which meant... "You offering us a place with you?"

"I'm just saying. Mountains, forests, and safety, all rolled up in one package." The Dire shrugged, not looking so casual anymore. "There's a cabin close to mine. It hasn't been used in years, but together, we could get it right homey before the baby came. It's set back in the woods but close enough to mine to get help when you need it. Private but safe."

Thaus blinked, unable to believe the offer laid before him. He knew his brothers cared for Ariel; he'd had no idea how much, apparently. "You'd be okay with a mated couple coming into your territory? With our pup running around?"

Phego met his eyes, the look he gave one of confidence

and truth. One of honor. "It would be a privilege to protect someone as brave as your mate."

Thaus didn't have an answer, but he didn't need one. As much as he appreciated the offer, this wasn't something he could jump into. Ariel would want to voice her opinion, and he'd give her that chance.

Still, his throat was tight as he answered, "I need to talk to Ariel first."

"Offer stands…today or two years from now."

Thaus wanted to say so many more things, to offer his thanks to his brother in a way he wasn't even sure the other man would understand. Ariel was everything to him. Always would be. For Phego to lay down his life, his privacy, that way—Thaus had no words for how grateful he was.

But before things got awkward or Thaus started blubbering, Ariel yelped loud enough for them to hear her in the hallway. Both men were crashing through the door into the operating suite before either could pronounce it was time to say fuck the rules.

"I'm fine." Ariel held out her hand, a preemptive move to calm her mate. "It hurt, but I'm okay."

"She refused the local anesthesia," Shadow said. He stood a good two feet from the bed, he and Deus both looking ready to defend themselves if need be. Thaus had his mate's hand in his, and she was smiling at him. His snarl wouldn't ebb, though. Not with males near her when she was so vulnerable. Forget who they were, his mind was only focused on what they were. Even Phego looked ready to kill someone, and he wasn't mated to the woman.

"Hi," Ariel said as she rubbed her fingers over Thaus' wrist in what could only be an attempt to calm him. "I'm chip-less."

"I like chip-less." Thaus coughed over his snarl, satisfied when it rolled down into a low growl. He leaned to press a kiss to Ariel's forehead, never letting Deus or Shadow out of his sight. "How's the precious cargo?"

Ariel's hand went to her still-flat stomach. "Safe and sound."

Thaus grunted and nuzzled into her neck, so fucking pleased that she was okay. He'd never let anything happen to her. Not again.

But his mate had other things on her mind. "How's your shoulder?"

He huffed a half-assed laugh. Of course she'd be worried about him. "You're the one on the gurney but you want to ask about my shoulder?"

Her voice softened, but her tone was determined. "I want to do this before we leave here."

As much as he hated it, Thaus nodded. She'd been pushing him for weeks to let her operate on his shoulder. Ariel was sure she could alleviate at least some of the pain and stiffness he dealt with, but Thaus wasn't sure he was ready to go back under the knife again. Besides, he'd been so focused on keeping her safe, the thought of being knocked out even for a few hours had been unbearable.

It still was.

"Only if all my brothers are here."

But Ariel was nothing if not stubborn. "Thaus—"

"No." Thaus kissed those soft lips he loved so much. "I can't risk you. Even being in the hall, with you just on the other side of the door was…"

He couldn't finish his thought. Couldn't find the words to tell her what he feared without breaking something inside himself. He couldn't risk her for a second, because the thought of losing her, just the thought, was enough to drive him straight into his long-neglected grave.

"You know, if you're having—" Shadow probably had some excellent advice or words of wisdom, but the shifter made the mistake of taking a single step toward Ariel. Phego's growl made the Feral Breed member go quiet quick. Even Deus backed up.

"Phego," Thaus said, snarling the word. He was ready to take his mate and leave. He needed her someplace safe, someplace where they could be alone. "End it."

Phego stepped to the end of the bed, placing himself between Ariel and Shadow. "She done here?"

When Shadow nodded, Phego moved to the other side of Ariel's bed and gave Thaus a serious look. "Let's get her back upstairs. This place is for sick people."

Thaus was definitely ready, but rolling Ariel through the halls of Merriweather Fields on a gurney simply wasn't going to happen. Shoulder be damned; he needed to hold his angel. So without thinking twice, Thaus lifted Ariel into his arms and cradled her against his chest as he headed for the door with Phego flanking him.

"I don't need to be carried, you know," Ariel said, sounding a little embarrassed.

Thaus didn't answer her. He also didn't put her down. His mate needed him, and he was going to take care of her. Even if she didn't like it all that much.

Though, he knew she really did. Ariel curled into his hold, safe and unafraid. Brave, like Phego had said. Her scars weren't healed by any stretch—there were still nightmares and moments of fear, anxiety attacks and the refusal to be close to certain people. But Thaus could deal with that. So long as she trusted him to take care of her, to keep her safe, he could handle anything.

And as Phego followed them up the stairs, as his brother guarded his six as only a true warrior would, Thaus leaned down to steal one more kiss from his mate.

"How do you feel about living in the Rockies?"

A *Dire Wolves* MISSION

Coming soon from *USA Today*
bestselling author
Ellis Leigh

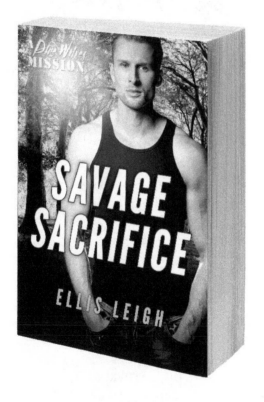

A *Dire Wolves* MISSION

Also
Available

FERAL BREED MOTORCYCLE CLUB
Claiming His Fate
Claiming His Need
Claiming His Witch
Claiming His Beauty
Claiming His Fire
Claiming His Desire

FERAL BREED FOLLOWINGS
Claiming His Chance
Claiming His Prize
Claiming His Grace

THE GATHERING
Killian & Lyra
Gideon & Kalie
Blasius, Dante, & Moira
Blasius, Dante, & Moira: Homecoming

About
the Author

A storyteller from the time she could talk, *USA Today* bestsellng author Ellis Leigh grew up among family legends of hauntings, psychics, and love spanning decades. Those stories didn't always have the happiest of endings, so they inspired her to write about real life, real love, and the difficulties therein. From farmers to werewolves, store clerks to witches—if there's love to be found, she'll write about it. Ellis lives in the Chicago area with her husband, daughters, and to tiny fish that take up way too much of her time.

www.ellisleigh.com